Praise for the writing of Cherise Sinclair

Club Shadowlands

"*Club Shadowlands* is a superbly crafted story that will dazzle any BDSM fan and have them adding it to their must read list!"

– Shannon, *The Romance Studio*

Dark Citadel

"Cherise Sinclair starts out using subtle skill to bring the reader into this exciting lifestyle. *Dark Citadel* is a decadent delight and an immensely satisfying read."

– Priscilla Alston, *Just Erotic Romance Reviews*

Breaking Free

"Ms. Sinclair is never disappointing. The author knows how to unlock your deepest passions with her characters."

– Tonya, *You Gotta Read Reviews*

"Ms. Sinclair has proved to me that she is a master at writing, drawing her readers in and keeping their attention throughout her story…"

Melissa C., *Fallen Angel Reviews*

"A riveting tale, *Breaking Free* is a book I highly recommend. "

Jennifer Bishop, *Romance Reviews Today*

Loose Id®

ISBN 13: 978-1-60737-618-7
BREAKING FREE

Originally released in e-book format in June 2009

Cover Art by Christine M. Griffin
Cover Layout by April Martinez

DISCLAIMER: Many of the acts described in our BDSM/fetish titles can be dangerous. Please do not try any new sexual practice, whether it be fire, rope, or whip play, without the guidance of an experienced practitioner. Neither Loose Id nor its authors will be responsible for any loss, harm, injury or death resulting from use of the information contained in any of its titles.

This book is an original publication of Loose Id. Each individual story herein was previously published in e-book format only by Loose Id and is a work of fiction. Any similarity to actual persons, events or existing locations is entirely coincidental.

Printed in the U.S.A. by
Lightning Source, Inc.
1246 Heil Quaker Blvd
La Vergne TN 37086
www.lightningsource.com

BREAKING FREE

Dedication

To my readers,

This book is fiction, not reality and, as in most romantic fiction, the romance is compressed into a very, very short time period.

You, my darlings, live in the real world and I want you to take a little more time than the heroines you read about. Good Doms don't grow on trees and there's some strange people out there. So while you're looking for that special Dom, please, be careful.

When you find him, realize he can't read your mind. Yes, frightening as it might be, you're going to have to open up and talk to him. And you listen to him, in return. Share your hopes and fears, what you want from him, what scares you spitless. Okay, he may try to push your boundaries a little—he's a Dom, after all—but you have your safeword. You *will* have a safeword, am I clear? Use protection. Have a back-up person. Communicate.

Remember: *safe*, *sane* and *consensual*.

Know that I'm hoping you find that special, loving person who will understand your needs and hold you close. Let me know how you're doing. I worry, you know.

Meantime, come and hang out with the Masters of the Shadowlands.

—*Cherise,* cherisesinclair@sbcglobal.net

Chapter One

Music, beer, tie up a willing woman, maybe use a flogger lightly…should be a no-stress evening. Nolan King leaned an elbow on the bar and took a hefty pull of Corona to wash the sawdust from his throat. With his paperwork finally caught up, he'd been able to go on-site and swing a hammer with his crew. Now his back and biceps had the muted ache of a good workout.

The edgy music of Nine Inch Nails from the dance floor mingled with the hum of conversation from the scattered sitting areas around the huge club room. Above the background noise came the sounds of BDSM play: the crack of a whip, a hand slapping flesh, screams and stern commands from one scene area. Just another Saturday night at the Shadowlands.

On the bar stool next to him, Mistress Anne, a tall, slender brunette in glossy red latex mini, sleeveless top, and black vinyl boots, handed her kneeling slave a bottle of water. She glanced at Nolan and patted his arm. "You're looking a bit tired, honey."

"Long day." *Good day.* The office building neared completion, right on schedule. A wail rose from a roped-off area, and Nolan turned to look. The sub being flogged on the St. Andrew's cross had finally been permitted to climax. Her sobs of relief continued for a good minute, and Nolan chuckled. "Raoul hasn't lost his touch."

"He's not bad at all." Anne stroked her slave's red hair. "We're up next, Joey. Finish your water. I intend to use you long and hard." Joey gazed up at her in adoration before lifting the bottle to his mouth and chugging the water.

"Aren't you monitoring tonight, Nolan?" Anne nodded at his black muscle shirt and leather jeans that lacked the gold trim designating a dungeon monitor.

"No. Z had enough people. I figure I'll grab a sub and put one of the upstairs rooms to use." Nolan glanced at the women sitting on the nearby couches. All were unattached submissives hoping to be noticed. Each had her own needs and desires. Finding one whose needs matched what he wanted to give was the trick and took not only good assessment skills but a willingness to communicate with the sub, before, during, and after a scene. Oddly enough, he'd come to enjoy the pre-scene negotiations: the mixture of attraction, flirting, and discovering the sub's wishes even while trying to uncover her hidden needs. Like constructing a house, a scene needed to be built from the ground up, starting with a solid foundation of trust. He snorted at the imagery. *Next he'd be writing poetry.*

"Really, Nolan, you should find someone a little more permanent. It's worth it." Anne smiled. When she leaned Joey's head against her bare thigh, the young man's nostrils widened as he obviously caught a whiff of his mistress's arousal.

"Been there, done that." Nolan returned to studying the subs. That little curvy blonde had potential. He liked soft under his hands. "I had a fulltime slave last year. Uncollared her before I did that consulting job in Iraq." He gave Anne a rueful smile. "Damned if it wasn't a relief. I don't like being a master full time."

Anne shrugged. "Some people don't. But a different sub every week gets tiring."

"Maybe." He glanced at the cross. "Raoul's cleaned up. You'd better grab the cross before someone else does. The place is busy tonight."

"This is true." Anne rose to her feet. She ran her fingers through her slave's hair and tipped his face up to take his lips in a demanding kiss.

When she stepped back, Joey rose to his feet and looked down at her, his lean muscles displayed by the leather harness.

She cupped his balls in her hand, curled her fingers around the jutting erection. "Let's see if you can last as long as Raoul's sub." Her fingers tightened enough to make the slave's muscles jump. "You won't disappoint me now, will you, Joey?"

"No, Mistress. Never."

Anne walked away, the slave following a step behind.

"That's one mean mistress." Cullen wiped a few drops off his gleaming bar top. "Glad my pride-and-joys aren't under her care."

Nolan snorted. "As if you'd put your balls anywhere near a Domme."

"Not in this lifetime." The huge bartender shook his head and grinned. "By the way, Z was looking for you. He's over by the chain station."

"Thanks." Nolan picked up his beer and rounded the bar to the left, heading toward a roped-off area midway down the wall. A few club members were watching the scene—a slender, redheaded sub, probably around thirty, with her arms chained over her head.

Seated on a couch nearby, the owner of the club looked up as Nolan approached. From the grim expression on his face, Master Z was in a mood dark enough to match his black clothing. He nodded at the adjacent leather couch.

Nolan sat and propped his boots up on the coffee table. "Problems?"

"A few." Z motioned to the chain station. "See what you think."

Nolan leaned back, sipping his beer. The redhead's arms had been shackled to the hanging chains but obviously not tight enough to jeopardize her sense of control. No spreader bar to keep her legs apart. Although obviously without underwear, she still had a corset and miniskirt on. *The scene sucked already.*

In his mid-twenties, the Dom didn't project much confidence. Even worse, he kept consulting a paper. What was with that? How-to instructions on topping? "What's he looking at?"

"Elizabeth has a few hard limits," Z said in a dry voice.

From what Nolan could see, her list of what she wouldn't do took up the whole paper.

The Dom spent a few minutes playing with her breasts, then used some ice and a spiky Wartenberg wheel without eliciting much response from the redhead. When he spun her around so her back was to the room, Nolan's eyes narrowed. Some major scarring there. Several wide scars. A few long ones from a single-tail. Shorter, precisely placed thin lines.

As the Dom turned the sub to face them, Nolan leaned forward. There were ugly, knotted scars on her right shin. The round shiny marks on her breasts suggested cigarette burns.

All the marks were white, so nothing had occurred within the last few months. Nolan's gaze traveled up her body to her restrained arms. More scars. "How bad are her hands?" he asked Z, his gut twisting.

"About what you'd expect from the rest. Old fractures, old burns. Puncture wounds in her palms."

Some bastard had played crucifixion games? "Hell, Z, have you killed the guy or are you saving him for me?"

Z rested his elbows on his knees, steepling his fingers. "It happened before she moved to Florida, and she won't discuss the Dom or her relationship with him." He nodded at the young Dom unfastening his leathers. "Can you see the problem here?"

Nolan took another sip of beer. The sub looked calm. Too calm, with her color even, eyes clear, muscles relaxed. No anxiety. No arousal from what he could see. The Dom's distress when he touched her dry pussy could be seen in the way his shoulders stiffened as he stepped back.

"Is she his sub?" Nolan asked, motioning toward the Dom. For all the synergy between the two, they might as well be on opposite sides of the club.

"No. She takes a new top every week with the same dismal results." Z sighed. "Elizabeth has a gardening service that she started about a year ago without any help. I hired her a couple of months ago, and she does a superb job."

"And this is leading up to?"

Z rubbed his eyes, looking tired. "She's a good person. Honest, full of enthusiasm. But when she gets here, she turns into a mouse. She's not just submissive; she's terrified. She comes to the club because she requires more than the vanilla world can offer, but we're not meeting those needs."

Nolan studied the scene some more. Pretty obvious what the problem was. She was too scared to give up control, but she needed to give up control to get her needs as a submissive met. "She wouldn't be an easy sub to top."

"Exactly." Z tilted his head. "You up to the challenge?"

As a boy, Nolan and his brothers had pretended to be Knights of the Round Table. Now Z had just thrown down a gauntlet. *Wasn't that nice.* Nolan scratched his jaw, thinking it over. He'd been back from Iraq for a few months now and had settled into his life. He had work he loved and good friends. Had subs and sex here at the club. Did he want more?

His gaze drifted back to the redhead. The Dom was working her clit and getting nowhere. Nolan shook his head. Nine-tenths of sex was in the head, and that little sub's head wasn't into the scene at all. What would it take? *First her idiotic list would have...* He stopped and scowled at Z. "You are one manipulative bastard, you know that?"

"Thank you, Nolan. Might I say, you're not an easy mark?" The corner of Z's mouth lifted. "You in?"

The club owner was smooth, sleek...and as easy to stop as a steamroller. "She has a Dom already," Nolan pointed out. "She might not want to change."

"I will handle that." Z rose to his feet and moved to a place outside the roped-off area where the young Dom would catch sight of him. Most of the people watching the scene had already left, lured to the next station down where Jake was caning a wailing blonde restrained on the spanking bench.

Leaving his beer on the coffee table, Nolan joined Z.

"Master Z." The Dom walked over, trying to not show any relief.

"Patrick, I hate to interrupt, but I wanted to ask you for a favor."

"Of course, Master Z." The Dom turned to check on the sub, and Nolan nodded approval at his conscientiousness.

"Our trainee, Sally, is unhappy that she scored poorly on a college exam, and I wish to give her a treat. Since she's enjoyed your use in the past, would you mind taking her under command tonight?"

After a second, the Dom reluctantly shook his head. He waved a hand toward the redhead. "I have—"

"No problem, Patrick." Z nodded to Nolan. "We were discussing Elizabeth a bit ago, and Nolan professed himself interested in a challenge. If you want to take care of Sally, he can relieve you here."

The young Dom was no idiot. "You're a sneaky bastard, Z, but I can see that I'm not the Dom she needs."

Z squeezed Patrick's shoulder, his face sober. "To be honest, Patrick, that Dom may not exist. But we'll try. Come, make your regrets and find Sally. She's expecting you."

As they walked over to the sub, Z said in an undertone to Nolan, "That's twice in five minutes I've been called a bastard. My mother would be extremely upset."

Nolan snorted. Despite being richer than God, Z's mother had a down-home sense of humor; the old woman would probably laugh her head off.

What was going on? Beth watched as Master Patrick talked with Z and a strange Dom. They all looked at her. Her uneasiness grew when Master Patrick picked up his toy bag before returning to her.

"Beth," he said. "Master Z has a suggestion for you."

A suggestion? She glanced at the bag filled with his BDSM equipment. "Are you stopping the scene?"

He nodded. "I'm sorry, but it's not coming together for us. Maybe this will work better." He gave her an apologetic smile. Beth's stomach clenched when he handed her limit list to the stranger before walking out of the scene area, leaving her still chained to the station.

She turned her gaze to the two big Doms. Master Z was impeccably dressed in his usual black silk shirt and tailored slacks. In contrast, the other Dom looked rough in black leathers and a skintight muscle shirt that showed off a powerful build.

Fear ran through her. Why had Z sent Patrick away? And why was that other Dom here?

Master Z studied her, then lips compressed; he shook his head. "Beth, I fear the Shadowlands is not the best place for you. I think—"

"No!" Horror rolled through her. He would kick her out? Cancel her membership? She'd have nowhere to go except the Tampa clubs where no one would watch out for her. She would have no real safety, would never be able to relax knowing Kyler could walk in at any time. Stupid to need this so much, but she did. "No, please, Master Z." She yanked at her cuffs, wanting to drop to her knees before him. "I...whatever you want, I'll do. Beat me if you need to—" *Beat her?* Just the idea strangled the voice in her throat. "No...I mean..."

He stepped closer, cupped her face with his hand. "Little one, you are not getting what you need here. I suppose we can try one more time, but you'd have to actually cooperate and give up some control. Can you do that?"

"I will. I promise, Sir." Maybe she didn't get everything she wanted from coming here, but it helped. Helped ease the stranglehold the coldness inside had over her emotions, kept it from growing and taking over her life.

"Then this is what will happen." He nodded to the sinister man standing to one side. Beth glanced at him, met unwavering dark eyes. His gaze captured hers, pinned her in place. She stared at him, barely breathing, before ripping her eyes away.

"Master Nolan will be your Dom tonight and in the future," Z said. "As long as he is willing to top you, you may remain. If he gives up, I'll terminate your membership immediately."

Have that Dom top her? Take her under command? Panic filled her as her carefully built world cracked, splintering like antique glass. "Master Z, please." She dropped her voice to a whisper. "Please don't do this. I don't like him. It can't—"

"Have you met him?"

She shook her head.

"Beth," Master Z said quietly, "I've known Master Nolan for years. I trust him. What's more to the point, I trust him with you." He tilted his head and waited for her answer.

Beth's breath hitched. Master Z didn't threaten; everyone knew that. It was one of the things that made him such an effective Dom. So either take the cruel-looking Dom at his side or leave forever. "I'll try, sir," she whispered, although her insides shook.

"Excellent." Master Z stepped back. "Nolan, your sub, Elizabeth."

She looked at the Dom. Everything about him seemed hard. Mean. At least six feet tall, broad shouldered, thickly muscled. His darkly tanned face was the reddish-bronze of Native American ancestry. His eyes were black. Reaching his upper back, straight coal-colored hair, exactly as long as hers, had been tied with a leather band. A long white scar ran over his left cheekbone. She winced, knowing exactly how that must have felt.

His menacing gaze ran over her slowly, inch by inch. He didn't miss anything; his eyes lingered on her scars, her breasts, her legs. At least she still had on some clothes, was all she could think. What would he do to her? If he whipped her, she'd leave. She'd have to leave. She bit her lip to hide its tremble.

"Physical problems?" he asked Master Z.

"None. Her medical forms state she's in good shape." Master Z gave her a fleeting smile and simply walked away, leaving her with this stranger.

"Spread your legs," he snapped, and she did, the panic wrapping around her and filling her head. He brushed a hand across her pussy, through the red curls, and grunted when his hand came back dry. He looked…brutal

Kyler was elegant, slim and smooth, and a *monster*. How much worse would this man be? A tremor ran through her.

He saw her reaction immediately; she had a feeling nothing escaped those piercing eyes. The authority and power that radiated from him demanded submission, and she dropped her eyes.

This was an experienced Dom, the type she avoided.

"Your safe word is red. If I think you're using it before you need to, I will stop immediately, and we will be done permanently." His deep voice sounded like gravel being poured out of a truck, his words taking on the impact of boulders striking the earth. Her shoulders tried to hunch, to prepare for the pain.

"You may use yellow. I will take it into consideration and may or may not stop. Look at me now." His eyes were cold, empty as a starless night. "Do you understand?"

"Yes, Sir." The quaking increased, expanding from her stomach and into her chest. She tried to ignore it. *She could do this.* She was in the Shadowlands, and there were people everywhere. They weren't alone.

"You may address me as Master, Master Nolan, or Sir." His lips twitched. "My Liege or Sire will work occasionally if you're trying really hard to suck up."

"Yes, Sir." A joke...or not? She couldn't tell, and that realization scared her to death. At one time, her survival had depended on the ability to read every nuance in a voice, every expression in a face. He gave her nothing.

"If I institute high protocol, you will keep your eyes lowered and speak only when permitted. However, during a scene I want your eyes on me." He tilted her chin up, met her eyes in a look that seared straight down to her toes. "You have pretty eyes, Elizabeth. Keep them on me."

A compliment? The flash of pleasure at his words disappeared as the sound of her full name engulfed her in the memory of Kyler and how his voice would thicken with anticipation. "*Elizabeth, you didn't... Elizabeth, you forgot... Elizabeth...*" She cringed.

Master Nolan's eyes narrowed, the pressure of his fingers increasing on her chin. "Your eyes," he said. A pause. "Pretty." A pause. "Elizabeth."

She didn't move when he said her name, she knew she didn't, but his head tilted slightly before he asked, "What would you prefer to be called?"

"Beth. Please call me Beth, Sir." Would he do that or would he prefer to punish her with her given name?

He nodded and released her. When he stepped back, she managed to pull in a breath.

"Normally we would discuss your limits, wants, and needs at this point in time." He glanced at her hard limit paper, tore it in half, and dropped the pieces on the floor. "The normal procedure obviously hasn't worked out for you." He lifted his eyebrows and waited.

No, no, no. She bit back the words. Took a breath. Another. Unable to speak, she managed a nod.

"My job is to give you what you need. We may not agree, so until I know you better, I will not gag you. What is your safe word?"

"Red, Sir," she whispered, the tremors spreading to her legs.

"Very good." He ran a finger down her face, his touch warm on her chilled skin. Grasping her hair in one big hand, he tilted her head back to take her mouth, not permitting any movement, and yet she didn't receive the crushing kiss she'd expected. Instead, his firm lips teased her mouth, and his tongue brushed over her lips until she opened.

He kissed her slowly, thoroughly, as if he had no plans to do anything else. Ever.

Pleasure fizzed through her like a shaken-up soda.

When he finally drew back, her lips burned and her head spun. No one had kissed her like that since…since high school when she and Danny parked his car and would kiss all night. After a second, she blinked back to reality and realized in amazement that she'd forgotten her fear for that time.

His intense gaze focused on her face. "You kiss well, sugar."

She had a second of delight from the compliment.

He ran a finger down her cheek. And then his hand continued down her neck, her chest. His fingers slowed at the whip marks, and a flash of anger appeared in his eyes.

When he stroked along the swell of her breasts, she stiffened. Would he touch her below now? Was he planning to whip her? She couldn't…

His fingers opened the front of her corset, tiny hook by tiny hook.

"No." The word escaped. She'd been naked before, but he was different from the other Doms.

One eyebrow raised, and his gaze stabbed her to silence. The corset dropped onto the wood floor.

His strong hands cupped her small breasts. He rubbed her nipples with his thumbs, and she found the sensation fairly pleasant. A corner of his mouth turned up. Abandoning her breasts, he unzipped her latex miniskirt and let it slide down her legs to the wooden floor.

Naked. Totally vulnerable to him. To *him*. Her hands jerked as she instinctively tried to cover herself.

As the chains restraining her hands jangled, he glanced up, then stepped back. He simply stood there, waiting, until her panic slowed.

She couldn't take her eyes off him. Now he'd touch her, try to bring her to—

He took a spreader bar off the wall, the widest one. Unhooking a set of cuffs from his belt, he buckled them onto her ankles and attached the bar, pulling her legs apart with firm hands.

So quiet. Unlike some Doms, he didn't speak at all. But he never stopped assessing her—his eyes on her hands when her fingers gripped the chain too tightly, on her body when her breathing faltered, on her face when she couldn't conceal the tiny quiver of her bottom lip.

Stepping back, he waited until… She didn't know what he waited for.

He winched the chains until her body stretched upward, her toes touching the floor just enough to keep the strain off her shoulders. She could move nothing now. Anxiety welled inside her along with the tiniest thrill. *He was totally in control.*

He grunted his satisfaction and circled her, coming to a stop behind her.

She flinched when a callused finger ran down her back, ever so slowly, and she realized he was tracing a scar.

"Metal-tipped flogger?" he asked, his voice casual. His finger slid down one mark, then the other, one by one until her skin began to anticipate the next stroke.

She nodded.

His finger brushed along her side. "One-tail?" he asked, continuing to touch her shoulders, her back, her flanks. Each gliding touch was light and excruciatingly slow. His fingers grazed over her bottom, and a quiver ran through her.

"Knife?"

"Yes, Sir." Kyler had boasted of the evenness of the cuts. All she could remember were her screams.

"How long were you with him?" he asked. Just a request for information.

The lack of emotion in his voice let her open the door to her memories a little further. "Two years." Two years of pain that had slowly buried her sexuality until she wasn't sure if Beth, the woman, even existed anymore.

Master Nolan touched each parallel scar. Other Doms occasionally asked a general question about the humiliating, ugly marks of Kyler's displeasure. She now knew he had hurt her for his own pleasure, not because of her actions, yet the scars still embarrassed her as if she'd been at fault, as if she were as worthless as he'd always told her.

No one had ever looked at each one, questioned each one. She felt like the Dom had pulled her out of the shadows where she'd been hiding, and instead of revulsion, she found only mild interest.

He stroked down her thighs, her calves. He walked to her front and started at her toes. Moved up, stopping at her right shin and the knotted scars there, the uneven bone beneath the skin. "What did this?" he asked, his voice a whisper.

"Cast-iron skillet, Sir."

Did he growl? He worked his way up, his stroke so light she barely felt it, and yet her skin grew so sensitive she was aware of the heat from his fingers before he even touched her.

His touch found the scars on her hip, the burns on her breasts, the healed gashes on her chin and cheekbones, the bump on her nose from the fist that broke it.

"Sugar, you're a mess," he murmured. His voice didn't ooze sympathy, just stated a fact. He took her lips again. Harder this time, deeper, but just as slow and careful. Velvet and iron. His tongue took complete possession before enticing hers in turn. Her breath quickened as a slow burn started low in her belly. She could go nowhere, refuse nothing. Could only submit. And enjoy. Slowly he pulled back, stopping to nibble on her now-swollen lips. He drew her breath into his lungs, gave her his, the exchange more intimate than sex with someone else might be.

His hands cupped her breasts again as he'd done before.

An unexpected tingle ran through her. She jerked when his abrasive thumbs rubbed her nipples. He tugged at one peak gently, rolling it between his fingers, his intent gaze on her face, her mouth, her eyes.

Incrementally, the pressure increased with each pinch, each roll of his fingers until an electric current sparked to life, flowing between her breast and her clit. Until her breath huffed in.

He kissed her again, his mouth demanding. One hand cupped her head to hold her in place, as the other stroked her breast. His kiss distracted her, and a sharp pinch to her nipple made her jump, hiss in surprise. He continued, drugging her with sensuous kisses, shocking her with pinches until her insides started to melt and a glorious feeling of arousal rushed through her.

She leaned into his kiss as his hands slid down her body, lower and lower, until he touched the curls of her pussy. He drew back and showed her his hand, his fingers glistening.

Her mouth dropped in disbelief. She was wet. How long had it been?

He licked his fingers, and his firm lips curved into a smile. The line of a crease in his cheek softened his face slightly.

"I like your taste." His blunt words eased the worry inside and warmed her. There were actually things he liked about her. And unlike the other Doms, he didn't appear frustrated or unhappy with her.

After glancing around, he walked to the wall and brought back a low stool, seating himself in front of her. His face was level with her crotch. For a minute…then another…for what seemed like an eternity, he just looked at the *V* between her legs where she gaped open from the leg spreader. His gaze burned into her, and she felt her labia, her clit, warm and awaken. When he finally touched her, she jolted and sucked in an uncontrolled breath.

His gaze rose, and he watched her face with those unreadable eyes as he moved his finger through her slick, wet folds. His finger, just one, slid slowly from her mound, down beside her clit, down almost to her anus, and then back ever so slowly. Again and again, he traced that route, as if he had nothing better to do, no plans to do anything else. Each unhurried stroke wakened more nerves until her lower body pulsed with urgency, until her hands fisted around the chains with the need to push against his hand.

He changed and moved his finger to her clit, circling but never making contact, the deliberately slow swirls making her restless in anticipation. Frustration. She could feel her clit harden, enlarge, then throb painfully when nothing, *nothing* touched it. She dampened further, aching for release, but he didn't seem to notice, this Dom who didn't appear to miss any little nuance of her movements. Another piece of her control began to slip away.

"Sir," she whispered. She hadn't been this close in so, so long. "Sir…"

His gaze darkened, and his mouth tightened to a severe slash. "You do not have permission to speak." And his finger never slowed. A circle, another, her clit on fire, her world narrowing to just his touch.

When he removed his hand and stopped touching her entirely, she whimpered.

In silence, he removed the spreader bar. Her legs closed over her engorged clit and swollen labia. Over her own wetness. Her body ached, needing more.

He unbuckled her ankle cuffs and removed them, reattaching them to his belt. When he rose, she stiffened, preparing herself, mentally and physically for the invasion of his cock. Fear and anticipation mingled together as her need died down to a simmer.

He held his wet fingers in front of her face. She could smell her arousal. "You will smell like that next time, sub," he said. "And possibly I will take you further."

Next time? Not now?

He released her chains. She would have fallen except for the strong arms that steadied her.

"Easy, sugar," he murmured in a deep growl. He drew her closer and cupped her bare bottom with his hands, pulling her up against his rock-hard body. A thick erection pressed against her stomach.

So he *did* want her. The knowledge sent desire surging through her, followed by anxiety. He wanted her; why didn't he take her? She looked up at him in confusion, met his unreadable black eyes, and watched those eyes crinkle slightly at the corners.

This time when he kissed her, his tongue moved in the same slow circling rhythm as his finger, reminding her of the sensation. And again, her lower half grew heavy with need, her swollen clit throbbing with every heartbeat.

Her legs wobbled. He tried to pull back, but her arms were tight around his neck. Even as she pressed herself to his body, she trembled. He must know how excited she was. He would bend her over, take her… He'd eroded her control, the shields holding her together.

Grasping her upper arms, he moved her away from him. His gaze ran over her as he checked her steadiness.

And then he tapped her cheek gently and walked away, leaving her naked and aroused.

Staring after him. Hating him. *Wanting him.*

Chapter Two

Beth managed to keep the previous night's events out of her mind until she reached the Shadowlands, her last job of the day. After she finished with the bed of ferns, she moved her kneepad under one of the live oaks and started weeding the caladiums. The heady scent of lush growth and rich earth enveloped her, filling her with contentment. She loved her work.

And this place. She glanced at the three-story stone mansion behind her. Of all her jobs, the Shadowlands was her favorite. God, she'd been so lucky to snare the yard service contract. In the right place at the right time… How often did that happen?

On her first night in the club, she'd heard Master Z complain that his gardens looked ragged. Shaking in her stilettos at the audacity of interrupting a Dom's conversation, she'd spoken up. Instead of dismissing her, he'd not only hired her, but threw in a club membership as part of her payment. Considering she wouldn't have been able to afford another month of the hefty fees, she'd been thrilled.

She edged a little farther into the shade as the sun's slanting rays burned her legs. Summer in Florida was so different from California. Both hot climates, but California was a dry sauna and Florida a very wet one. She glanced at the black clouds building in the sky and heard the low rumble of thunder, a warning of the daily afternoon downpour to come.

A bird swooped past in a flutter of wings, probably heading for one of the fountains scattered throughout the Capture Gardens. She leaned forward, patiently working her way through the bed, piling weeds beside her.

Weeding was a nice routine chore that left her plenty of time to think about how frightened she'd been last night. She could still feel Master Nolan's fingers stroking her so intimately, and her response… A shiver ran through her.

For the first time in a year, she'd felt truly alive, none of her emotions frozen. She'd felt like a woman, something she wanted and needed, but not from someone like Master Nolan. He was too experienced, too powerful. He wouldn't permit her to retain any defenses.

And although she didn't judge people by their appearance, his rough looks frightened her. His cruel face actually made Kyler look sweet. She stared at the puncture scar in the center of her hand. *Kyler wasn't sweet.*

Her mouth twisted, and she pushed aside the ugly memories. *Stay in the present.* She pulled another weed and tossed it onto the growing pile. Why did ripping plants out of the earth feel so satisfying? Because she could restore order to at least something in her life? Have control over one thing?

She sure hadn't been in control last night, not after Master Z had sent Patrick away. Master Nolan had been totally in charge. He hadn't asked her what she wanted or needed. Nothing. Too much like Kyler...only not quite.

Just wanting to hear her scream, Kyler had only been interested in her response to pain. She didn't know Master Nolan's goals, but he'd watched her response to *everything*. He'd seen when she began to panic, but he hadn't offered comfort like other Doms or changed his plans. He'd just waited her out.

She could hate him a little for that.

She definitely hated him for leaving her so aroused that she'd whimpered. How could she be so thrilled to have actually felt desire and so humiliated at the same time? Sitting back, she pulled her legs up and laid her head on her knees. *God, she was a mess.*

"Hey, Beth."

Beth jerked her head up and looked around to see Jessica walking through the garden's gate. The pretty blonde in khaki shorts and a golden top looked crisp and cool, a far cry from Beth's mud-stained appearance.

"I saw your truck and trailer. Don't you ever take a day off?"

"Now and then. The Shadowlands has such extensive gardens that I'm here almost every afternoon except Saturdays when I'm getting ready to play and Fridays when..." She grinned. "Much to our mutual embarrassment, I discovered that your swinging crowd shows up early on Fridays."

Jessica laughed and sat down on the nearby stone bench, avoiding the iron rings embedded in the sides where a sub could be restrained. "They're sure enthusiastic. Z keeps threatening to drag me there, but he's kidding." A frown creased her brow. "I *think* he's kidding."

Beth huffed a laugh. She'd never met anyone as difficult to read as Master Z. Jessica was a brave woman to have him for her Dom. Then again, Master Nolan had been just as impassive. Nothing in his face had revealed his emotions. "How well do you know Master Nolan?" she asked before she could stop herself.

"Nolan? Not that well." Jessica leaned back, tipping her face to the sun. "He and Z are friends, but he just got back a few months ago from Iraq and apparently has been occupied with catching up on his business."

Keeping her face averted, Beth leaned forward and tugged out a volunteer impatiens. "Isn't he a bit old to be playing soldier?"

"Z said… Let's see…" Jessica thought for a moment. "Right. He had a military contract as a consultant for construction or engineering or something. He was only gone a year." Jessica leaned forward and stared down at Beth. "You're not planning to ask Nolan to top you, are you? I mean, you always seem to like the less exp… He's not an easy-going… Uh, I'm digging myself into a hole here, I think."

"You didn't get to the club till late last night, huh?" Beth gave her a rueful smile.

"Yeah. Cullen said you'd been in and left. So did you meet Nolan?" Curiosity gleamed in Jessica's green eyes. "Tell me, tell me."

Beth hesitated. It had been a long, long time since she'd had someone to really talk with, not since she married Kyler, and he'd systematically cut her off from everyone. Did she even know how to be a friend anymore?

"You don't have to tell me anything, you know," Jessica said gently. "But I get lonely for girl talk sometimes; no one in the vanilla world really gets what BDSM is all about." And that was as open an offer of friendship as Beth had ever received.

"I take it Master Z didn't mention me." Beth pulled a dandelion carefully, trying to get the entire long root. Master Z didn't allow herbicides. "He said Nolan would top me in the club, and if that didn't work out, he'd cancel my membership."

Jessica blinked in shock. "He can't do that."

"He can." Beth shrugged, although her heart warmed at the outrage in her new friend's eyes. "No, don't go yell at him. He wasn't trying to be mean. He wanted to help; I know that. It's just...Master Nolan's a bit scary." And wasn't that the understatement of the year.

"Oh, please, that's like saying Hannibal Lector only eats low-carb meals."

Beth felt a giggle escape her, then another when Jessica rolled her eyes, and then she was really, really laughing.

Tears filled her eyes, not from the laughter, but from the bittersweet joy rising in her. So she still had some emotions besides fear left; Kyler hadn't killed all the bright ones.

* * *

Saturday night, Beth walked through the open doors of the Shadowlands, head high, shoulders back. Although her stomach was in knots, she knew her appearance was adequate. Since Kyler had been out of town when she'd run, she'd had time to load her car with her clothes and the few mementoes he hadn't broken. Most of it was totally unfit for a lawn service, but, hey, she had some nice fetish wear.

Tonight, she'd tried on every last piece before settling on a golden PVC bustier with matching short skirt and thin golden wrist cuffs. Would Master Nolan approve? People said the color brought out the highlights in her red hair, but she never felt very pretty. Not anymore. God knew Kyler hadn't found her attractive. *Titless, bony, stick-figure, dead-fish white.* She'd known he liked hurting her, and still the derogatory comments battered down her ego as inevitably as the ocean turned cliffs into rubble.

She felt like rubble sometimes, but she wouldn't let him win. No way. Tonight she had gazed in the mirror and knew she looked all right. Even if she couldn't really believe it.

"Good evening, Miss Beth," said the guard standing behind the desk.

"Hi, Ben," she said. Ben was so big and ugly and sweet. He reminded her of Andre the Giant.

He grinned. "Nice outfit."

The compliment was a stake propping up her sagging confidence. She beamed at him. "Thank you."

He checked her off the membership list and waved her toward the door to the bar. As she stepped into the main club room, the ambience of the Shadowlands washed over her, pulling her into its lure. In the right corner, the dance floor churned with people, mostly the younger crowd moving to London After Midnight's music. Later in the night, Z would change the music to slower tunes, easing the mood down.

The circular bar loomed in the center of the room like a massive mahogany ship with the bartender, Cullen, at the helm. Scattered around the bar were sitting areas with leather couches and coffee tables, some hidden behind plants and low walls. Beth headed for the area where single subs tended to congregate, a place near the bar where the Dom/mes could look them over and vice versa.

Spotting Beth, a plump blonde sub waved, her long nails sparkling in the light from the chandeliers. Looking down at her own hands, Beth winced. Despite the lotion she continually rubbed into her skin, her hands still had the roughness of a gardener. She rubbed her fingers together, felt the calluses, and sighed. The scent of strawberries and lemon came to her, improving her mood. One of the few things she'd left behind had been the heavy, musky perfume that she'd hated. Now her lotion might make her smell like something good to eat, but it never failed to make her smile.

Beth approached the group of subs and then hesitated. What did Master Nolan expect her to do? Sit and wait for him to find her? Or try to search him out? She knew, with a sinking feeling, whatever she did would be wrong. That's how it always worked. What kind of punishment would that harsh Dom inflict?

When a painful pang ran up her arm, she realized she was wringing her hands, twisting fingers smashed a couple years ago. The memory of that agony filled her head like an oily black river, dragging her deeper. Helpless.

She turned as sickness rose into her throat. She couldn't do this. He'd hurt her, and she—

She ran right into him, slamming into his muscular body like a bird hitting a mountain. Master Nolan's hands closed around her upper arms, steadying her. Unable to breathe, heart pounding, she tried to wrench away. He held her easily, his fingers like metal clamps around her arms, but not tight, not painful.

"Gently, sugar." His rumbling voice surrounded her, strangely calming.

She managed a deep breath, then another, before looking up. No anger showed in his face or, even tougher to disguise, in his eyes. Patient as a stalking cat, he waited for her to get her act together.

Some act—she'd lost control completely and panicked in the middle of the bar. "Please forgive me, Sir," she said to her feet. "I..." Her voice trailed off. What could she say?

Releasing her arms, he tilted her chin up with his fingers until she had to meet his gaze. "You lost your nerve for a minute"—his eyes studied her—"and now you are all right."

Not a question, just a statement, but she nodded anyway.

"You look good in gold," he said.

She blinked. A compliment? Maybe he wasn't as inhuman as she'd... She looked down. "What are you doing?"

"What does it look like?" he asked evenly, his scarred fingers slowly unlacing her bustier. Her hands rose, and she forced them back down to her sides, although she couldn't keep her fingers from curling into fists. He finished, and the front of her bustier flapped open, displaying her breasts.

His hand curled around her arm, holding her in place so he could run his other hand over her exposed skin, right there in the center of the room.

Her chin tilted up as she forced her expression to show nothing. He'd get his jollies, and then they'd get on to business.

"Very pretty breasts," he murmured, his black gaze on her face. "You're a little underweight, and we'll discuss that later, but I like touching your nipples. The pink is the color of your lips. Look, don't you agree?"

Forced by his understated order, she tipped her face down and saw his hand hold one breast up. He circled the pink nipple with his thumb. His dark skin against her whiteness was startling. *Erotic.* Suddenly, she felt every little roughness on his thumb, the warmth of his palm under her breast. His thumb rubbed against her peaking nipple, and the sensation zinged right down to her crotch. Her stomach muscles tightened.

She jerked her head up, trying to school her face back into no expression.

Satisfaction flickered in his eyes. "Come, sub." He curved an arm around her waist and started walking toward the front.

Her hands pulled the bustier front together.

"Leave it open. I will be playing with your breasts off and on this evening." His words made something inside her tense and curl into itself.

He took her to the food tables and set a thick turkey and ham sandwich in her hand without taking anything for himself. “Eat that.”

At the crowded bar, he pulled her against his hard side and waited silently while she ate. Too nervous to eat supper earlier, she discovered her appetite had returned…as long as she didn’t try to think about anything that might happen tonight. As long as the Dom was quiet. Within a few minutes, she’d actually finished the whole thing and earned herself a “Good girl.”

The place was busy, not that the bartender moved any faster. Master Cullen worked at his own pace. By the time he strolled over to take their order, Beth had grown comfortable with Master Nolan’s arm around her waist, with the feel of his solid body against hers, the sound of his deep voice as he talked with other Doms.

“Evening, Nolan. Got yourself a redhead tonight?” Cullen leaned an elbow on the bar and grinned.

“Pretty, isn’t she,” Sir answered.

Her? Pretty? Beth closed her eyes for a second to savor the compliment. This pitiless Dom wouldn’t bother trying to butter her up, wouldn’t bother to lie. He meant it.

“I’d have to agree.” As the bartender’s gaze traveled over her, she grew way too conscious of her exposed breasts. Why did that bother her? She’d been fully nude in front of people before. But she’d never felt so…naked.

Nolan watched the color rise and fall in the sub’s cheeks, her lips no longer tight but soft. Vulnerable. Her fragility worried him, not just her mental state but the physical too. She was only skin and bones. He preferred pillowy women with ample mass to cushion his big body, with soft hips to grip. Beth had no padding, and he'd need to be careful.

Nice breasts, though. What he'd call perky. Keeping her trapped against his side, he ran his hand over her nipples again and smiled as they came to little points. She'd left her hair loose, and the dark red strands danced over lightly freckled shoulders left bare by the bustier. The freckles ran down past her collarbone then faded away, leaving her breasts a creamy white.

He'd thought of her often over the past week, trying to figure out the best way to deal with her. And he'd decided he needed more information before anything else could happen.

Cullen set a Corona down for him, and glanced at the sub. "Beth?"

Nolan looked at her in surprise. If Cullen didn't know what she drank, then she'd never ordered anything in here. Interesting. "Tell Master Cullen what you would like."

"I don't need a drink," she said and added a belated, "Thank you, Sir."

"Do you have a problem with alcohol?"

"No, Sir." She was back to staring at the floor. "I just prefer to have all my senses."

"I prefer you have a few less. One drink only and you will finish it all." He grinned when her little fists clenched and released for the second time tonight. So there was still a fire burning down there. The asshole who'd damaged her hadn't wiped that out. "Cullen, bring her a screwdriver."

When the drink came, Nolan handed it to Beth and led her to a couch. He took a position at one end. She started to kneel, and he stopped her. "Sit beside me. We'll leave high protocol for another time." To be clear, he added, "I will tell you when I want it observed. You won't have to guess."

Her mouth relaxed slightly, just enough to tell him she'd been disciplined before for guessing incorrectly about...probably everything. Some Doms kept their requirements impossible to meet so they had an excuse to mete out punishment. He might say he didn't work that way, but he could see she didn't believe a Dom's words. Her trust would have to be earned. His gaze ran over the scars on her breasts; she had good reason for fear. He patted the cushion beside him and, as she sat down, slid her closer until her thigh touched his. Her fragrance drifted to him, a hint of strawberry and lemon, pleasingly light compared to the heavy scents of the club.

He nudged the drink toward her lips, watched her take a sip before pleasing himself and taking her breast into his hand again. Odd how satisfying her little breast was, perching like a dove in his palm. And like a captured dove, she froze in his grip. Under his fingers, the tiny thud of her heartbeat accelerated. He ran his thumb over one of the shiny burn marks. "You were with the bas—person who did this to you for two years, right?"

She stiffened, her mouth flattened into a line, so he waited. She didn't seem to know how to deal with patience or silence. The asshole must have been both impatient and a shouter.

Her tongue wet her lips. "Yes, sir."

"Long time." Bet it seemed like a lifetime. And from the way her muscles tensed, she wouldn't willingly discuss that period. Another item they'd work on later. *Hell.* Topping her was like walking blindfolded through a minefield. "Drink," he growled, and she started.

She took a sip.

"How often do you masturbate?" he asked.

She choked, and red stained her cheeks.

He smothered a smile. In the lifestyle for years and still modest? Amazing. "Answer me, sub."

She took a hefty swallow of her drink. "I don't." After a second, she managed to look him in the eye. She had lovely eyes, the color of the turquoise jewelry his mother collected.

"Why not?"

The red deepened. Normally he enjoyed seeing a sub flush, but this was almost painful.

"I… It didn't… I couldn't get off, and I can't explain why."

But oddly enough, he could understand. He'd come to a few conclusions about her. He figured her last relationship started off well, even with good sex, but as it turned ugly, she'd probably shut down her response to pleasure as well as pain.

Could her arousal be dependent on being dominated? "Could you orgasm before those two years?"

"Yes, Sir."

Good. "Was that just from masturbation or also with a man? And, if so, what kind of men?"

Her brows, thin arches of reddish-brown, drew together.

"What?" he asked.

"This isn't what I expected. Questions. Talking."

"A conversation of sorts?" Nolan ran his fingertips along her jawline, noting the stubborn set to her chin despite the delicate bones. "Didn't any of the other Doms talk with you?"

"I…" She stared down at her hands. "They tried. I didn't want… I just wanted to get started." She glanced up at him hopefully.

He stomped that hope to dust. "Not gonna happen, sugar. You're going to learn to talk to me. Answer my questions."

"Yes, I could get off with men before," she snapped, then turned dead white, flinching away from him.

Leaning back, he set his boots on the coffee table and took a slug of Corona. He'd almost forgotten he had the damn drink. "I'm not going to haul off and hit you, Beth. During a scene, I expect proper respect. During a conversation, as long as you refrain from outright rudeness, I will tolerate more." He smiled and toyed with the half-curls touching her shoulder. Apparently the fiery glow of her hair was matched by her spirit. "It's rather fun to see you flare up. What kind of men got you off?"

Chapter Three

"Well…" How in the world was she supposed to answer that? Beth frowned.

Master Nolan took her hand and held it despite her efforts to pull away. "Big men? Gentle men? Doms or vanilla?"

"Beth, you're here!" Attired in a tight blue latex dress, Jessica trotted up and leaned over the back of the couch. "I'm glad you made it. Do you want—"

Master Nolan didn't even look up. "Jessica. Go away."

"Sorry to interrupt," Jessica said brightly without moving. "I haven't seen Beth, and I wanted to talk to her for—"

"Silence." Master Nolan's face turned cold. Mean. Eyes widening, Jessica took a quick step back.

He lifted his hand, and a trainee hurried over. "Sir?"

"Fetch Master Z immediately."

"Yes, sir." The sub ran. Beth would be running too if the Dom looked at her like that.

Master Z must have been at the bar for he appeared within a minute. "Is there a problem?"

"Your sub interrupted, spoke to my sub without permission, and ignored my order to leave." Master Nolan's ruthless gaze flicked over Jessica, returned to Master Z. "Deal with her."

Master Z's jaw tightened as he heard the offenses. He hadn't even looked at Jessica. Now he asked Master Nolan, "Do you wish to participate?"

Master Nolan snorted. "I have enough on my plate."

"She was just worried about me," Beth said. She couldn't let Jessica be hurt for trying to help. "That's not fair that—"

Master Nolan's gaze settled on her like black fire. "Be silent."

Her tongue froze in her mouth.

"Please send for Jessica later so she can apologize properly," Z said to Master Nolan. Z's gaze when it settled on Jessica was enough to chill Beth inside and out.

Face pale, Jessica took a step back. "Sir, I didn't—"

Z shook his head, and Jessica closed her mouth, biting her lip until it turned white. After locking her cuffs together, he pulled her away, heading toward the stockade. His voice trailed back, "Since you enjoy annoying Doms so much, I think we'll let the Doms show their appreciation."

Beth touched Master Nolan's wrist and dared to say, "Sir, she was just trying to help me."

His cheek creased as if he almost smiled. "I know. And I wouldn't have pursued the matter if she'd left when ordered. But she's not only loyal but also foolish." He put a finger under the glass she held, lifted it toward her mouth. "Finish that before it's undrinkable."

She drank it down, and a slight buzz hummed through her veins. Cullen made strong drinks.

"Tell me about the men you've been with."

"You are so tenacious." She huffed in exasperation, shocked when he laughed rather than slapping her to the ground.

He'd actually laughed. God, he looked different when the coldness disappeared. The sun lines around his eyes crinkled, a crease appeared in his cheek, and he was… Her world shifted sideways, leaving her dizzy. She could *not* be attracted to him.

"How long were you in the lifestyle before you met the asshole?"

"Not very long." She tried to remember something that seemed a lifetime ago. "A month or two?"

"So you'd been with a Dom before you met the asshole?"

"Two." He made a *give me more* motion with his fingers, so she continued. "The last one had been a Dom for maybe a couple years, and he was nice. He took good care of me."

"You got off every time?"

"About half." Kyler had seemed so much more dangerous, so thrilling in comparison to sweet Andy. And the sex with Kyler had been wonderful at first.

"Tell me about the other one."

Her lips curved. "He enjoyed teaching new subs, and he was very strict. No backtalk, only 'Yes, Sir.'" Her smile grew at the thought of him. "I think I tested every limit he set, kind of like Jessica does."

"And what did he do for punishment? Are any of those scars from him?"

"No, he never did anything to break the skin." The thought would have appalled Master Chris. "Spanking, paddles. A flogger or cane once in a while. He embarrassed me once, and that was horrible." She winced inside at the memory, and then added, "But I've done so much since then that I don't embarrass easily."

"That's good to know," he said. After setting his beer down, he lifted her onto his lap as if she didn't weigh a pound. With unyielding hands, he leaned her back until her head rested on the arm of the couch, her body across his thighs, and her legs on the seat cushions. Her bustier flopped open, leaving her breasts pointing up in the air. After licking his finger, he ran it around her nipple.

Her face heated. What was he *thinking?* Indignation rolled through her. Scenes belonged in the roped-off areas. In those locations, her mind was steeled for being in public, and her body prepared. But sitting here in the middle of the bar being treated like a toy doll? No, this was just wrong. Her hand came up to push him away, and he looked at her, waiting for her to do just that. She set her arm carefully back at her side.

"Good girl." His voice warmed. He ran his big hand across her breasts and down her stomach in long, slow strokes as if petting a cat. "So, with the strict Dom, how often did you climax with him?"

"Every time. Sometimes even when I didn't expect to." She sighed. The happy memories felt so distant, glowing somewhere on the horizon, nowhere she'd ever be again.

"And with the bastard, how did you fare, orgasm-wise, with him?"

Somehow it was getting easier to talk with him, maybe because of his lack of reaction to whatever she said. Just that intense attention. His hand caressed her breasts. "At first, really good. And later, not at all."

"As the pain got worse."

"Yeah." She breathed in and dared to ask, "So what happens tonight?"

"I haven't decided yet," he murmured. "I had a long day, and it feels good to get off my feet. I like having you stretched across me, offering me your breasts. And your mouth." He bent to take her lips, harder than he had last week, taking possession, demanding her tongue back. He drew the kiss out, nibbling on her lips, before plunging back into her mouth. No hurry, no urgency. Just firm lips against hers, the plunge of his tongue, the slight scrape of his beard shadow.

Her body warmed as his scent engulfed her, soap and leather and a hint of masculine musk. His hands moved over her breasts slowly, massaging, circling the nipples. Then he took a peak between his fingers and sent jolts of pain/pleasure through her.

By the time he drew back, her breathing was ragged, and her hands were clamped onto his rock-hard biceps.

He glanced down at her pleated PVC skirt. "Nice skirt." His hand ran up her leg, under the skirt. When he discovered the bikini briefs she wore, his brows drew together. "Lift your hips up."

She did, and he yanked the briefs down to her knees. “Lift your legs.”

Acutely conscious of where they were, she raised her feet so he could slide the briefs off. She started to lower her legs.

“Leave your knees bent. And, Beth, don’t wear underwear to the club again. Am I clear?” The implacable gaze returned to her face.

“Yes, Sir.”

“Good. Any time I am not clear in my instructions, you are permitted to ask.”

She nodded and then froze when he flipped up her PVC skirt to expose her completely. She felt like a piano; his left hand playing with her breasts, and his right… His right hand moved up her leg and settled against her pussy.

“Sir, this isn’t a scene area,” she told him as if he didn’t know. This just wasn’t right. She glanced around to see if anyone—

“Keep your eyes on me, sub,” he said, pinching her nipple, and hot desire ran through her as if her breasts and clit were connected by high-voltage wiring. Lower down, her nerves flared to life as his sure fingers slid through her folds. When had she become wet?

His fingers circled her clit, never touching, and the nub began to throb. This was too much like last week. How did he do this to her?

With his left hand under her back, he lifted her, bringing her breasts up to his mouth. His right hand rubbed gently over the hood of her clit as his hot, wet mouth sucked her nipple. She trembled as hot need flared like lightning inside her, turning her insides molten.

His finger grazed over her clit, once, twice, and her core constricted.

He went back to stroking her folds. *Oh, God, she needed more.* Her mound tilted up into his hand. "Very nice, sugar," he murmured. When she managed to focus on his face, he was smiling.

"Open your legs farther."

She didn't want to, really didn't want to. Her fear had disappeared, oddly enough, but lying across his lap felt wrong. Too intimate. Scene play was more focused and less personal, at least when she had her way. The Dom would be standing and doing stuff. She shouldn't be sprawled half-nude on a Dom's body.

"Beth." He drawled with a faint southern accent, the warning clear.

She moved one leg. An inch.

As his brows drew together, her foot crept to the very edge of the couch cushion. And as the movement opened her slick folds under his hand, he pushed his finger into her, hard and fast.

"Aaah!" The nerves inside her flared to life for the first time in years. Shocked, she arched her back, and he bent his head to take her nipple in his mouth as if she'd offered her breasts to him. He bit gently on the tip.

The sharp stab of need sizzled all the way to her pussy, and she tightened around his finger. When he sucked on her nipple, the pulling sensation squeezed something deep inside her.

He slid his finger in and out of her vagina, and his thumb angled to slip over her clit. The rhythmic sensation was impossible to ignore, coordinating with his sucking and biting on her nipple. Tension coiled inside her as her body swept out of her control. Her entire lower half burned. Every touch sent her higher and higher. She grabbed his arm, her fingernails digging into his wrist, needing something, anything to hold on to.

He paused, and little mews of need escaped her. He started again, driving into her forcefully, his thumb directly on her clit. Her thighs trembled as her muscles stiffened and held. Another fierce plunge, another stroke of his thumb over her clit and the room sheeted to white, a fireball of sensation exploding inside her. Pleasure sizzled through her nerves.

His thrusts didn't stop. As her hips bucked, his left arm turned to a vise around her, holding her for his touch as he wrung every last spasm from her.

Damn, she was a gorgeous sight when she came, Nolan thought, his hand over her pussy, his finger still deep inside her. As her eyelids fluttered shut, her muscles went flaccid. He'd known she was tense, but not how extreme it had been until now when the stiffness flowed right out of her. He bent to lick her nipples, soothing the red marks his small bites had created. Each time his tongue touched her, her pussy twitched around his finger.

There was nothing as fulfilling as having a woman come apart in his arms, and this little sub had badly needed to get off. And more. Her scream of release had echoed with pain. He'd breached the barriers she'd erected to keep people out.

He hadn't expected she'd trust him enough to let go. Not yet. But she was submissive, through and through, and dominance, not pain, was her key.

Sliding his finger from her body won him a low moan and blinking eyes. "Sir?"

Well, now that felt good; her unthinking acknowledgement of his mastery even before her brain turned back on. He flipped her little skirt down and gathered her up so her head rested against his chest. Her breath created a warm spot on his T-shirt.

Over the background noise in the club, he heard footsteps approach. Z stopped in front of the couch, a subbie blanket over his arm.

Nolan grinned and nodded, thinking that the Shadowlands owner should be called *Father Z.* Z tucked the blanket around Beth and left without saying a word.

She burrowed closer, her head fitting nicely in the hollow of his shoulder, and he caught the faint scent of strawberries and lemon. She was so light; he could hold her all night without a problem.

So he slid down on the couch, leaned his head back, and enjoyed the simple contentment of having a snuggly, satisfied sub in his arms.

She woke to the rumble of conversation around her, hearing men's voices before she was quite awake. Where was she? A body shifted under her. A man's arms were around her. She froze, her breath stopping as panic surged through her. Kyler. Memories flooded her mind, how he'd hold her lovingly after whipping her for hours.

With a thin wail, she pushed away from him, rolling off his legs, and landing on her butt on the floor. She scrambled backward, breath heaving, seeing only men's legs around her. She'd woken to a nightmare.

"Stop." A command.

Her muscles froze.

"Beth, look at me."

Panting in terror, she looked up and into dark, dark eyes. Not pale blue ones. *Master Nolan.* Her arms almost collapsed as relief flooded through her. She licked her lips, tried to speak, and nothing came out.

He simply pointed to the floor beside his feet. His face showed no reaction or anger, as if subs panicked and fled from his arms every day.

Her bustier gaped open as she crawled back to him, the wooden floor hard and cold against her knees. She knelt next to his legs, keeping her eyes down. He must be furious. Her insides shook so violently that her stomach twisted, and she swallowed hard. Carefully she placed her trembling hands palms up on her thighs. She closed her eyes, tried to breathe, tried to remember where she was. Florida. The Shadowlands.

Master Nolan.

After a minute, he pressed her head against his solid thigh, letting her rest there. And he stroked her hair lightly. Little attentions, nothing special, the sort any Dom might give a sub to let her know he wasn't upset, to let her know that he hadn't forgotten her.

Nothing special, dammit. Yet the feel of his gentle hand on her hair made her eyes burn with tears.

She kept her eyes lowered, blinking fast, and the conversation continued around her. Master Z's voice. The bartender, Cullen. Another Dom…maybe Master Dan? They were discussing upcoming activities. Theme nights. The Fourth of July. The Dom's monthly meeting at the Palms Restaurant.

"So when are you going to start having your play parties again, Nolan?" Cullen's voice. "I've missed them."

BDSM parties? At Sir's house? As the implications of that registered, she stiffened.

And he could feel it. The hand that had been stroking her hair tilted her chin up. "Don't worry, sugar. You'll have fun."

No question as to if she'd attend, just the simple assumption she'd bow to his will. He lifted his eyebrows and waited.

Here in Florida, she had never, ever done a scene anywhere but the public areas of the Shadowlands. Never dated. Never used the private rooms upstairs. Do a play session at someone's home? She shivered. But others would be there, right? So it wouldn't be too much different than doing a scene here in the club with others present. She wouldn't be alone with a Dom. With him.

"Yes, Sir," she said finally.

He nodded as if he'd known she'd comply, and yet his "brave heart" was like a splash of warmth.

But the room still felt cold, and the tremors inside her were working their way out.

His hand stilled on her hair. With a firm grip, he pulled her between his legs and wrapped the blanket around her, tucking it securely beneath her knees. His legs against her sides felt like hot iron bars.

A trainee sub appeared in response to some motion, and Sir said, "Bring me a hot chocolate."

When the hot chocolate appeared, Master Nolan put it into Beth's hand, waiting until he was sure she wouldn't spill. She sipped, and warmth flowed through her, heating her inside as surely as his surrounding body heated her outside. She felt enclosed and safe between his legs with his hands resting lightly on her shoulders. She finished the cocoa and set her cup on the floor.

As the conversation flowed around her, she dared to rest her head against his leather-clad leg. When his hand stroked down her hair, the sigh she gave was of perfect contentment.

For this moment, this moment only, no fear intruded.

* * *

He stepped into the BDSM club in downtown Tampa, grimacing as the music of Velvet Acid Christ assaulted his ears. Two sluts, drenched in nauseating perfume, lined up behind him. As the fat one chattered away in a shrill voice, he could almost feel his favorite cane in his hands and how he'd whip it across her insipid face and split the thin tissue of her lips. Blood would splatter the wall and drip down onto the glossy pink latex corset she wore.

"Sir."

He blinked, shook his head.

"Sir," the doorman repeated, holding his hand out for the fee and shoving a clipboard forward. "Sign here, please."

He scrawled his name, *Kyler Stanton*, taking his time so he could check the list. No Elizabeth Stanton. No Elizabeth at all. But he couldn't assume she wasn't inside.

She might be clever enough to use an assumed name. Anger coiled in his stomach, a growing monster biding its time before bursting free. He'd given her his name, one of respect and dignity. If she'd abandoned it as easily as she'd rejected his home—and him—her punishment would be quite severe.

* * *

Nolan had sent Beth home an hour before, her nerves obviously overloaded. She'd done better than he'd anticipated. Of course, she still didn't trust him worth a damn. Taking a sip of beer, he twisted on the bar stool to watch the scene at the St. Andrew's cross. A Domme was doing sensation play, running a feather up the inside of her sub's legs. The poor guy was trembling, his shaft pointing straight up. If he got off now, his cum would probably hit the ceiling.

Nolan grinned. Mistress Anne would have locked that cock in some metal cage and added weights. Amazing what a difference there could be between Dommes.

And that brought his thoughts back to Beth and the Doms she'd known. He understood her wariness. After her experiences, she wouldn't trust *anyone* easily, especially a Dom. He sighed. The edge of fear was where trust could be engendered, but if he tried to push her there, she'd flee. Catch-22.

That little sub was definitely a piece of work. He scratched his jaw. On a work site, cement trucks tended to empty unused dregs on the ground, sometimes right in the way of something else. So the crew had to shatter the heavy concrete mass and then dig it out. What tools could he use to break up the ugly mass of memories in Beth's mind? It wasn't going to be easy or quick.

Holding his beer, Nolan wandered through the room. This late at night, the club was quieter, although most of the stations were still occupied. At the stockade, a burly gay Dom in biker leathers paddled a willow-thin sub who groaned with every slow stroke.

Farther down, at the lacing table, a Domme indulged in wax play with an older blonde whose breasts were covered with white streaks. The sound of the sub's moans as she approached her peak almost killed Nolan. His cock had been throbbing like a sore tooth since he'd touched Beth's wet pussy.

Nolan turned and went the other direction, finally taking a chair near the suspension station to watch Cullen play with Sally. The trainee sub was in her mid-twenties.

With a golden tan, long, curly hair the same rich brown as her big eyes, and a very soft, full figure, the sub was a pleasure to fuck. A bit mouthy, too smart for her own good, but thoroughly submissive once a Dom got past the attitude.

Totally focused, the bartender worked a flogger up and down the pretty brunette with nice rhythmic strokes, alternating the pressure, sometimes hard, sometimes soft. As Sally's cries changed, showing she couldn't differentiate the pain from the pleasure, the flogging moved from her curvy ass and thighs to lighter erratic blows on her ample breasts and pussy. Her eyes glazed, her breasts and hips arching to meet the blows.

Before Sally could come, Cullen stepped back, nodded in satisfaction, and unfastened her, steadying the sub when her legs wobbled. A hip-high bench stood nearby—Cullen was always prepared—and now he laid Sally on her back with her head dangling off the top. Her ass jutted out over the other end. Cullen bent her legs up and strapped them against her waist. Top and bottom open and ready for use.

After glancing around, Cullen walked over to Nolan and tossed a condom in his lap. "Why don't you come and play? Sally's never had it from both ends, and she's been a good little submissive all night…as good as she ever is. And you've been a good boy too; everyone in the place heard Beth scream as she got off. Nice job, but you're probably ready to explode."

That was the truth. Nolan picked up the condom and eyed Sally. She quivered as she craned her neck, trying to see where Cullen had gone. Her frustration was obviously growing by the second, and Nolan laughed. "Looks like we'd better get over there or she'll come without us."

"Be a nice change. I think she's been faking it with some of the newer Doms." Cullen frowned. "Maybe I'll talk Z into giving a workshop on detecting fake orgasms."

"That'd be interesting." Nolan grinned, thinking about Z's sub who really hated doing public scenes. "Jessica will hide under the bed if she hears you suggest that one."

Cullen's roar of laughter silenced the whole club for a second. Still chuckling, he motioned to Sally. "Let's go play. If she fakes it, I get to beat her some more."

Nolan snorted. "After the flogging you gave her, she'll explode the minute we get in her."

Cullen eyed the flushed sub. "Looks that way." Unfastening his leathers, Cullen walked back to the bench. "Dibs on oral."

"Works for me." Moving to the foot of the bench, Nolan opened his leathers, getting a rush as his aching cock sprang free. A good Dom put a sub's needs first, and Beth hadn't been ready to be fucked.

This one was.

Her arms were strapped at her waist, her legs folded up and out of the way. Nolan nodded his approval of the restraints. He ran his hand over Sally's pink-striped ass, making her moan. "Sally. What is your safe word?"

Her gaze settled on him, then his cock, and her eyes widened as she realized he was planning to take her. "Red, Master."

"Use it if you need to, Sally," Nolan instructed. "There will be two of us, so you might need it."

Her eyes widened. Her breathing increased, her dusky nipples pebbling.

Cullen grinned at Nolan. "She likes it on the rough side."

Nolan grunted a laugh. The way he felt, that wouldn't be a problem. With a ruthless smile, he massaged her tender butt, tracing every welt the whipping had left while Cullen did the same with her breasts. It wasn't long until her breathing turned ragged, and her hips tried to lift despite the straps. "Please, Masters, please," she whimpered.

"Okay, love. Since you ask so nicely…" Cullen said and angled her head. He looked down her body at Nolan and nodded. Both men thrust into her at once, filling her mouth and her pussy. The sub arched upward, her vagina clamping on Nolan's cock, spasming around it so violently he almost came right then. She screamed, the sound muffled by Cullen's cock.

She was panting so fast that Cullen pulled out and waited, his hand around his cock. Nolan moved slowly in and out of her, enjoying the pulsing around his cock as her aftershocks slowly died.

With a sigh, she relaxed back on the bench. She looked up at Master Cullen. "Thank—" He filled her mouth with his cock before she could finish and nodded at Nolan.

With long experience, Nolan timed his moves to Cullen's, waiting until Cullen started to pull back, and then Nolan would thrust into the snug little pussy. One, then the other, just slowly enough that the nerves would barely recover before the next thrust. He could feel her pussy start to tighten.

"I love this bench," Nolan said. "It's just the right height." He slid his fingers through her folds, making her jerk. After tugging on her swollen labia, he circled his fingers around her clit, just teasing until her hips strained to lift. Then he pushed her, rubbing harder, increasing the speed of his thrusts.

He grinned, watching her try to focus on serving Cullen as her arousal grew, and her climax approached. She finally gave up, breathing too hard to suck cock. She was very close to coming. Five, four, three, two… Nolan slammed deep into her, pinched her clit and held.

She climaxed powerfully, her shrill cries throttled by the cock in her mouth.

After jerking back, Cullen glared across the bench. "She bit me. Warn me before you set her off."

Nolan chuckled. Sally reminded him of those firecrackers that would explode in quick snaps, one after the other. Nolan studied her flushed face. Wasn't she a pretty sight? Maybe she should have one more since she'd been such a good girl. "You ready, sugar?"

She nodded and tipped her head back. Cullen pushed his cock back into her mouth, and Nolan saw her working it steadily, taking it deep.

Nolan gave her a little time to relax, then leaned forward, reangling his cock and watching her face as each of his thrusts hit a different place in her vagina. Suddenly her eyes dilated, and her pussy quivered. He nodded. *Right there*. He started hammering her with short, fast strokes, each one slamming into that place inside.

Her legs strained against the straps, the muscles in her thighs quivering. Her pussy clenched, her whole body going rigid. Nolan said to Cullen, "Consider yourself warned."

The Dom snarled and pulled out just as Nolan set a finger down right on top of her overstimulated clit and pressed.

"Ah, ah, ah, aaaahhh." Unmuffled this time, her screams rolled through the club. Her pussy rippled around Nolan's cock as her hips made futile bucking jerks against the straps. As her climax lessened, the little sub's whole body shuddered.

"You know, I really don't get the impression she's faking." Nolan glanced at Cullen. "You get bit again?"

When Cullen growled, "You're such an asshole," the sub's eyes widened. She tilted her head up, obviously terrified she'd nipped Cullen's cock.

Cullen barked a laugh and tugged on her hair. "I pulled out, love. Now open up." When she opened her mouth, he thrust into her again.

Nolan's strokes were slow and easy as Cullen's became stronger. Sally dropped her head back farther, letting him deep-throat her. A few more strokes and Cullen's face grew flushed. He looked at Nolan. "Let's do it."

Nolan started thrusting in unison with Cullen, fast and deep. As the sub's pussy constricted around him, his balls drew up. They were pounding into her so hard, she grunted with each thrust.

When Nolan stroked a finger right beside her clit, and Cullen pinched her nipples, the sub's whole body went rigid, and she keened, the sound blurred by the thick cock in her mouth.

Nolan smothered his laugh at the sound of the sub's wail. He knew she was close even without the telltale tightening around his cock. His cock was straining to release, the urge becoming all-consuming. Increasing the pressure, he stroked her clit in rhythm with his thrusts. Her high wails turned into shrieks as she went over.

As she convulsed around him, he gripped her hips, holding her so securely that his fingers dug into her soft flesh. He pumped into her with short, intense strokes and finally let himself come, his cock jerking so hard with the release that his vision blurred.

Across the bench, Cullen gave a bellow as he got off.

Nolan felt the sub's legs still quivering in his grip. Her wails had diminished to moans of satisfaction. He slid in and out gently, enjoying the rippling aftershocks milking his cock. As he started to pull out, he glanced down at Sally's clean-shaven pussy and thought of Beth's soft folds, her slickness on his fingers.

How would it feel to bury himself in Beth's pussy and see those red curls surround his cock like a glowing fire?

Chapter Four

She'd had an orgasm. During the week that followed, Beth couldn't keep her brain from circling back to that, over and over. As she mowed lawns, trimmed bushes, cleaned up debris. As she fertilized, sprayed, and weeded. As she designed and planted new flowerbeds.

Now, late Friday afternoon, at her apartment complex's pool, she balanced on the diving board and dove in. She surfaced with a gasp of pleasure, the water cool against her overheated skin. The faint scent of chlorine mingled with the fragrance of banana and coconut suntan lotion wafting from the women on the lounge chairs. They fluttered and chattered like a flock of birds, casting flirtatious looks at the two men at a nearby table.

Beth sighed. She'd had so much trouble finding a furnished apartment in a decent area that she'd resigned herself to a singles-only complex. But she didn't belong here with these carefully made-up women who never got in the water. She felt like a common daisy planted amidst orchids.

But as Beth finished her laps and sat on the pool's edge, she realized she felt pretty today. Last week, a man had looked at her, at all of her, and shown his pleasure. Had obviously enjoyed touching her. She glanced down at her suit, at her almost nonexistent cleavage. The *girls*, as a friend like to call her breasts, seemed to sit a little higher, appear a little perkier. And if that wasn't the dumbest thing she'd ever—

"Hi."

At the sound of a man's voice, Beth turned so quickly she almost fell into the water. Heart pounding, she looked up. One of the men from the table loomed over her. Lanky, nicely tanned, hair carefully styled.

"Hi," she answered, pressing a hand to her chest. Being so panicky was liable to give her a heart attack one of these days.

"I'm new here," he said, holding his hand down to help her up. "My name's Todd."

"I'm Beth." She let him pull her to her feet, his hand soft, lacking calluses. When had she started to find a rough hand attractive?

"Want to join me and my friend? We're just hanging out, unwinding from work."

"Uh, no, thanks." She went through this about once a week. Her answer never changed. "I've got other plans." *Taking a shower, heating up some soup, watching TV.* "But thank you."

"That's too bad. Maybe next time." He smiled, then his eyes widened as he noticed the scars showing around the edges of her very concealing black suit.

She shrugged. "Nasty car accident," she said, lying without any remorse whatsoever.

An hour later, back in her tiny furnished apartment decorated in one-color-fits-all beige, Beth stared sightlessly at the car chase on the television. Tomorrow was Saturday. She'd see Master Nolan again. Her heart did a slow somersault inside her chest

She wanted to see him with an urgency she hadn't felt since meeting Kyler. Kyler who she'd been convinced truly loved her.

She'd been so very wrong.

Her hand tightened on the mug of tomato soup. She dreamed of Master Nolan every night, of his sure hands moving on her body, of the intense look in his eyes and how he saw her every reaction. In her dreams, her body would warm, arousal shooting through her... And then his face would blur into Kyler's. The sound of his rough voice would meld into Kyler's refined one. She'd hear the snap of the single-tail and then her grunts of pain when he shoved himself into her dryness.

Oh, God, what was she doing?

At one time, she'd loved Kyler so much she hadn't seen past his movie-star good looks to the monster inside. But if she could be so wrong about him, she could be wrong about anyone. There was no way to tell who a person was inside.

And although Master Nolan hadn't hurt her, he easily could. He was a Dom. Someone who wanted control. Complete control. She couldn't give him that. She didn't trust him...or herself.

She took a sip of her soup and had to force herself to swallow. Nolan had done what she'd hoped for. He'd made her feel alive again. And she'd felt something besides fear.

But he demanded too much. She was relinquishing too much of her control over her body…and her emotions. Her body might survive, but… She sighed miserably.

Before Kyler, she'd been tough, as sturdy as kudzu. You could jump up and down on the invasive vine, and it would just keep growing. After Kyler? Now she felt like an impatiens—step on it even gently, the stem would break, and it would die.

Her hands curled around the cup of soup, trying to absorb the warmth as cold grew inside her. Being with Master Nolan again was just too big of a risk. She needed to back away. But how? And what would Z do?

Pursing her lips, she considered. What if she got someone else to top her tomorrow? If that worked out, then Master Z wouldn't cancel her membership, would he?

And Master Nolan wouldn't want her if she humiliated him by obviously preferring another Dom.

She thought of his black eyes, his ruthless face, and shivered.

* * *

As twilight gathered around him, Nolan hammered one last nail into the board before rising to his feet. He rocked back and forth on his tiny dock—the structure no longer swayed under his weight. Good. One less chore on his list. His place had sure gone to hell while he'd been gone.

After wiping the sweat from his forehead, he sat on the end of the dock and listened to the background hum of his world. Water lapped softly against the wood. An egret flapped slowly overhead, a flash of white in the dark sky. A barred owl gave a series of hoots from the trees farther down. Around the water's edge, crickets trilled, and frogs chirped with the occasional bass note of a bullfrog. Near the center of the lake, a fish jumped, splashing back into the water.

In the desert, he'd craved the sounds of Florida, the feel of the humid air moistening his skin, the rich tropical scents with the underlying odor of sulphurous water. It felt damned good to be home.

Even if that home was empty.

He glanced back at his big house, designed and built to hold a family. Last year, he'd been happy to release Felicia, and she deserved to have someone who loved her more than he had. And someone who enjoyed being a full-time master. But he was fucking lonely at times.

As if summoned, his cell phone rang, the jarring noise silencing the frog chorus for a moment. He glanced at the display. His oldest brother.

"Hey, Adam, how's it going?"

"Life's good. Ah...you doing okay?"

A corner of Nolan's mouth turned up at the careful concern. During the years in covert ops, Nolan had been a damn fine killer, but it had taken its toll, and his brutal, bloody nightmares had terrified his family. Adam undoubtedly knew that Iraq had reawakened his ghosts. But Nolan had put them back to rest. Eventually. Being home was good. Getting little redheaded subs off was even better. "I'm fine, bro. Stop worrying. And how is everyone?"

"Not bad. Jenny's pregnant again. One more kid for the clan gathering."

Nolan grinned. His youngest sister wanted a big family; this would be her third. "I'll have to give her a call. How about you? Getting married yet?"

"Hell no. Not till they let me have at least two wives." A pause. "You still into the bind-em and beat-em stuff?"

Nolan snorted. "Coming from someone who prefers four or five people in his bed, you've got no room for snide remarks."

"Least I don't have to tie them up to fuck them," Adam said, continuing the long-running insult fest. "You gonna make it home this summer?"

"Probably not until fall. Why?"

"Dad wanted you to—hell, speak of the devil. He's on the other line. Talk to you later." Adam clicked off.

Nolan grinned and shoved the phone back in his pocket. Always good to hear from family. Sometimes he missed living closer, but considering his *perverse* lifestyle, distance wasn't a bad thing. He'd taken Felicia with him for a visit once. His mom and sisters hadn't taken to her. Even though she'd behaved appropriately, she was submissive through and through, and the King women were all hell on wheels.

What would they think of Beth with her myriad of scars? He grinned. Yeah, they'd like Beth. Although beat-up, scarred as all get-out, and terrified, she'd not only had the guts to escape but managed to start up a business in a strange city all by herself. They'd respect that.

Hell, *he* respected that.

* * *

That night, Kyler strolled up to the big stone mansion set in the middle of nowhere. Quite a place, he thought, admiring the fancy ironwork and the black sconces set on each side of the open door. He stepped inside.

"Good evening, sir." Behind a desk in the entry, the young man attired in a guard uniform rose as Kyler entered. A pretty boy, Kyler sneered inside, giving him a friendly nod.

"May I have your name, please?"

"I'm not a member of the Shadowlands," Kyler said, smiling. "An acquaintance mentioned she really liked the club. This is a BDSM club, right?"

"On Saturday nights, yes. Tonight is swing night."

Wrong night. Hell. "Any chance of seeing the place…maybe tomorrow, since I'm into BDSM?"

The guard shook his head. "Sorry, sir, but only members are allowed inside."

"What does it take to be a member?"

"There's an open house twice a year for people wanting to join. Otherwise a current member must recommend you. If you have more questions, you can call Master Z at this number." The guard handed over a black card with Shadowlands inscribed in a raised gold font.

Kyler's jaw flexed. An exclusive club for the well-to-do. Surely she wouldn't be a member here. But he hadn't found any sign of her in the open Tampa clubs. "Can you tell me if my friend comes here? Elizabeth or Beth? Slender redhead with big blue-green eyes." Vulnerable eyes that filled with tears so easily. A husky voice whose screams he heard in his wet dreams.

The guard started to nod, then visibly caught himself. "I'm sorry, but our clients value their privacy. I cannot confirm that one way or another."

"I understand completely." Kyler kept his expression calm and interested despite the sense of victory flaming inside him. *Got you, you bitch. I've got you.* "Well, I'm sure I'll catch up with her sooner or later. Thanks for your time."

"No problem. Have a nice night."

Kyler walked out into the night, his stride loose and even, his posture straight as he'd been taught. And all the way to his rental car, the delightful screams of his wife echoed in his head.

* * *

On Saturday, Beth greeted Ben, laughing at his jokes despite her anxiety. As she entered the Shadowlands, she spotted Jessica and waved, moving through the crowd toward her. The scent of perfumes, men's colognes, leather, sweat, and sex filled the air. She dodged a Domme berating her slave and walked around a couple entranced by hot wax play at a station. A flash of blue flickered against the rafters; someone was playing with a violet wand at the far end.

She pushed past two more people, finally reaching Jessica. The little blonde was wearing a hot pink camisole with a tight black latex skirt. "You look great," Beth said with a sigh. When God was handing out breasts, Jessica must have been at the front of the line. And Beth would have brought up the tail end.

"Forget that. How are you doing?" Jessica asked, grasping Beth's hands. "Are you all right? What happened with Nolan?"

Beth smiled, gave up any hope of reticence, and hugged the other woman, pushing down a forlorn desire to beg her for advice. "I was going to ask you the same thing. What did he do to you?"

Red streaked Jessica's skin. "That evil bast—" Her gaze focused on a point over Beth's right shoulder, and she choked.

Beth spun, almost colliding with Master Z.

His face showed nothing, but his silvery eyes danced with laughter. "Yes, little one, tell Beth. What did the evil *bastard* do?" Master Z crossed his muscular arms over his black silk shirt and waited.

After giving him a nervous look, Jessica focused on Beth. "He put me in the stockade, flipped up my skirt, and let any Dom passing by have a whack." Her mouth tightened. "Some of them came back for seconds and thirds. I couldn't sit down for two days."

Remorse surged through Beth so strongly that her eyes filled. Jessica had been hurt because of her. If she—

"Oh, heavens, don't you dare cry. It wasn't your fault; it was mine. I have a bad habit of not being properly respectful"—Jessica gave Master Z a rueful smile—"and sometimes the evil Dom calls me on it."

He stepped forward and brushed a kiss on top of Jessica's head. "And the bastard enjoyed every whack you got. I will be at the bar. Come directly there when you and Beth finish talking."

"Yes, Master." Her eyes soft, she watched him walk away, before giving Beth a wry grin. "He enjoyed watching so much that he took me right there in the stockade, damn him."

Beth bit her lip, remembering Jessica rarely did public scenes. "Sorry."

"Oh, he made sure I enjoyed myself. Only that makes it more embarrassing, and he knows it." Jessica shook her head and frowned at Beth. "Okay, now about you..."

"I'm fine. Really." Beth looked around the room, expecting to see Sir. She'd noticed people rarely crowded him, so he should be easy to spot. "Is Master Nolan here?"

"He's monitoring the dungeon for a while. One of the DM's had to leave.

The disappointment bubbling up inside her strengthened Beth's resolve to find a different Dom. And if he were busy, then she wouldn't have to talk to him. Once he saw her with another Dom, he'd be angry enough to blow her off without her having to try to explain why she couldn't continue with him.

Jessica's eyes narrowed. "What are you planning?"

"Nothing that I don't always do. Find a top for the evening. Have a little fun. Go home." Beth kept her tone light.

"And Nolan? What about him?"

"He got me off, so that block I had is gone. Life should be good."

"You figure he'll agree with that?"

Beth saw a Dom at the bar give her an assessing look. She smiled, pulled her stomach in, and pushed her breasts out. "If I don't want Nolan to top me, what can he do?"

"Nothing, I guess," Jessica said doubtfully. "But I can tell you that underestimating the masters here can be very painful. Good luck, hon."

"It'll be fine. You'll see."

Chapter Five

Nolan strolled through the big rock-walled dungeon room, keeping an eye on the various scenes being played out. Mistress Anne had her slave manacled to the wall and was adding weights to the studded parachute ball-stretcher.

An older gay couple was using the sling, and the Dom had trussed his sub's legs to the chains in an inventive way. Interesting. Before moving on, Nolan automatically scanned the sub. *Not good.* Clicking on his flashlight, he waved the beam across the floor to catch the Dom's attention, then on the sub's bluish hand. The Dom didn't speak, just went to work loosening the restraints. Nolan nodded and continued circling the room.

On the far side, he stopped to watch Heath, a Dom in his mid-twenties, trying to tie Sally to the bondage table. Heath was a conscientious Dom but perhaps too nice for the mouthy trainee. From the unimpressed look on her face, Sally needed a more controlling top. She was actually instructing Heath on where to place the restraints.

Nolan smothered a smile and then shook his head. From the look on Sally's face, she'd spend tonight provoking Heath to their mutual dissatisfaction. Not a good match there.

Relationships were relationships, whether vanilla or BDSM. All required a lot of looking before a person found someone who clicked. Maybe Dom/sub couples verbalized their requirements more openly, but searching still took time and effort. Hopefully pretty Sally would someday find a Dom who could meet her needs. Considering that her stubbornness rivaled her intelligence, she'd require one powerful Dom to master her.

He grinned, remembering the night he'd topped her. His hand had hurt by the time he'd finished spanking her. A fun evening, but as a submissive or a lover, she lacked that essential spark, at least for him.

Now with Beth... There was something compelling about the little redhead. Not the pain she'd endured, although he respected her courage in not letting it stop her. What really pulled at him was her vulnerability. She could have turned bitter and nasty to protect herself. Instead she'd built defenses to hide the softness underneath.

Formidable defenses. How the hell had he let Z talk him into taking her on? Snorting a laugh, he headed back toward the other side of the room.

Anne's sub was sweating like a pig, so Nolan snagged a bottle of water from the back table and left it at the edge of the Domme's scene space.

The clock read 11:30. Had Beth arrived? If so, why had she not come to find him?

Across the room, Dan appeared in the door and scoped out the area. Typical cop. The DMs here included a fair number of law enforcement types and ex-soldiers. In his usual black vest and leathers, the man crossed the room to Nolan. "Anything I should know?"

"All quiet." Nolan nodded toward the gay couple. "Got involved and had the restraints too tight."

"Uh-huh," Dan said, and Nolan knew he'd monitor the couple carefully. Like most Doms, Dan was overprotective to the point of absurdity.

Nolan handed over the flashlight. He tossed his gold-trimmed vest into a cubby to pick up later and pulled on a tight, sleeveless black shirt. "You seen Beth?"

"Ah." Dan turned his head, apparently mesmerized by Heath's rope work. "Yeah. She's...ah...doing a scene."

Found another Dom, had she? Nolan's hands closed until the knuckles cracked, and then he relaxed, amused at his own blindness. He should have anticipated something like this. He'd undermined her defenses last week, so she'd want to shore them up as hard as she could. "They got a station?"

Dan nodded.

She'd be easy enough to find. And if another Dom managed to get her to respond, more power to him. He rather doubted it would happen, not with that wary little sub.

He nodded to Dan and left the dungeon. As he walked down the long hallway of theme rooms, giggles and shrieks came from the playroom, groans from the medical room, and laughter from the office. Out in the main room, the stations near the door held two gay couples vying with each other for how long their subs could delay getting off. One of the two corner cages held a brunette with tears on her cheeks; someone had been bad.

So where was Beth? Nolan checked the roped-off areas down the right wall. No little rabbit. As he crossed the room past the bar, Cullen waggled a bottle of Corona at him.

"Thanks." Nice and cold. Nolan took a couple of swallows. "Where is she?"

Cullen nodded to the other side of the room. "Sawhorse. Bad choice of top. He's letting his frustration get to him."

"Hell." Nolan strode across the room. A small crowd watched as the beefy Dom hammered into the slender redhead restrained on the bench. Small grunts escaped Beth as the thrusting continued. Her forehead was pressed to the leather cushion, her hands clenched into fists. Just enduring.

Nolan wanted to grab the clueless Dom and shove him through the nearest wall, but that wouldn't be right. Beth had a safe word and was obviously nowhere near subspace or too frightened to use it. Her choice.

Bad choice, as Cullen had said. Nolan looked around. On a couch beside the rope barrier, Z watched the scene, his jaw set in a rigid line. Nolan joined him.

"I find this extremely painful," Z said.

"To watch or to feel?" Nolan asked. An open secret in the club, the Shadowlands owner was not only a psychologist, but could pick up emotions if close enough to a person.

"Both." Z sighed, rubbed his face. "I'm trying to decide whether to tear up her membership papers right here and now or wait until I'm less angry."

"She's a piece of work, all right. I'm a bit pissed off myself." He watched as the Dom climaxed, his face red with exertion, and his expression ugly with annoyance at the lackluster scene. Yanking himself out of Beth, he tossed the condom in the garbage and headed toward the paddle lying under the rope barrier. From the redness of Beth's ass, the Dom had already used it once.

Nolan walked over to the rope. The Dom picked up the paddle and, as he straightened, his gaze met Nolan's. Nolan shook his head and unleashed a little of his anger. "Finish. Now."

The paddle dropped, and the man took a careful step back. As he returned to Beth, his rigid posture shouted that he wasn't intimidated. Nolan didn't give a shit what the Dom did to salvage his pride. Compliance was all that mattered, and the incompetent bastard was unstrapping Beth from the bench.

He rejoined Z on the couch.

"If you and Jessica keep this up, I won't have a Dom left in the place," Z murmured, his lips quirked in amusement.

"Don't bullshit me. If I hadn't stopped him, you would have." Nolan kept his eyes on Beth. She pushed herself to her feet, face very pale. She was trembling but waved away the Dom's half-hearted attempt to help her. The Dom glared at her and stalked away.

"She could well drive a man to drink, but I'm going to have to keep an eye on him," Z said. "He doesn't appear to handle frustration well." He lifted his hand.

A trainee in loincloth and chain harness hurried over and actually knelt at Z's feet. "Yes, Master."

"Austin, please put up a reserved sign on the station and have Peggy clean it."

"This one will—"

Z interrupted, leaning forward and gripping the sub's chin. "Austin, *this* one prefers lower protocol be observed in the club. You don't kneel unless the Dom indicates otherwise. And the proper response is, 'Yes, Sir.'"

The sub actually quivered. "Yes, Sir," he whispered. Once back on his feet, he dashed away.

Nolan snorted and returned to watching Beth as she struggled with lacing up the front of her latex dress. Everything in him wanted to help her. He diverted himself by asking Z, "Got the trainees kneeling now?"

"Heard that, did you?" Z sighed and rubbed his eyes. "His master was into very high protocol. The relationship is terminated, but Austin still has that mindset. And I am quite tired of hearing 'this one' every few minutes."

"I enjoy high protocol occasionally, at least for the silence, kneeling, and lowered eyes, but not the third person bullshit." Nolan shrugged. "To each his own."

As Beth finished lacing her dress, he forced himself to lean back, set a boot on the coffee table, and drink his beer. A rescue on his part would only compound the problem they now had. She had to take the first step this time.

Finally finished lacing her dress, Beth pulled it straight with an effort. Her hands, her legs, hell, her whole body shook. Like a new planting in a strong wind, she felt as if she could be uprooted and blown away any moment. Her bottom and the backs of her thighs still burned from the paddling. The Dom had been very angry with her lack of response.

Her fault, she knew; it was always her fault. God, her emotions were wobbling almost as bad as her legs. Staring down at her feet, she bit her lip hard and forced back the tears. She took a long, calming breath. *All right then. Time to go home.* She looked up—and straight into Master Nolan's black eyes.

Her body jerked back as if he'd hit her, her breath exploding from her lungs.

He was right there. On the couch. He'd watched the awful scene. Oh, God. She wanted to run from the room, from the club, and never come back.

He didn't move. And then he tilted his head, lifted his eyebrows slightly in a way that said she hadn't lost everything with this horrible mistake...if she had the courage to acknowledge she'd been wrong.

She could, for once, actually read his expression. Her hands curved into fists, pulling at the new cuts where she'd gouged her fingernails into her palms. She couldn't move. If she went to him now, her decision would be voluntary, not coerced by Master Z's threats. This time Master Nolan would demand she submit with her whole heart, not just her surface actions.

Could she do that?

She managed one step forward, then another. Her body felt unfamiliar, as if her legs belonged to someone else. She made it past the ropes, past the few people remaining. Their whispers brushed her ears. Her eyes never left Sir's.

And then she stood in front of him and couldn't think what to do next.

He waited, sipping his beer, his gaze steady.

When her legs trembled, and she almost fell, she recognized the next step. Such a simple one. *Such a hard one.*

She knelt at his feet. After a minute, she managed to tear her gaze away from his unreadable eyes and look down at the floor. The words came to her lips without her prompting, left her lips in a whisper. "Please, Master…"

"Aw, hell." The *thud* of a beer bottle being set on the table, the *creak* of the couch, and then firm hands grasped her around the waist. He picked her up effortlessly, set her on his lap, and pulled her firmly against his broad chest. When his arms came around her, the strength in them so obvious and so controlled, she shuddered, unable to form a coherent thought.

"Sir?" She struggled to sit up, to explain, to apologize.

"Rest now, sugar. We will discuss your idiotic behavior later." And the hint of laughter in his voice was like a warm spring shower on a parched garden.

The little rabbit quivered in his arms for quite a while before succumbing to sleep. Made Nolan feel good that she could relax enough to sleep in his arms. Twice now. They'd made progress, after all.

That or he just bored her senseless. As she snoozed, he watched Z's cleaning lady disinfect the bench and area before removing the RESERVED sign.

A married couple and their sub used the station next, the male sub receiving a well-administered caning with marks carefully placed up his thighs and onto his buttocks. A bit obsessive, that husband with the evenness, but the force was well calculated, sending the sub to a good place. After a bit, the wife took the sub's place and also got caned. Then she was double-teamed by both the husband and sub to everyone's delight. The wife was quite a screamer.

In his arms, Beth stirred at the noise, her muscles stiffening, but this time she didn't do a dive off his lap. Another sign of progress. She lifted her head, blinked sleepy, blue-green eyes, and stared at the scene area where the husband was unfastening his wife.

"You were asleep," Nolan said helpfully.

"I'm sorry, Sir. I didn't mean to…to use you…ah—"

"For a pillow? Guess you owe me then." Nolan grasped her hair, tilted her head back, and took his payment, a long, soft kiss from a sleepy woman. Been a while since he'd shared his bed, and he'd missed that small pleasure. He took it deeper, using his expertise to rouse her, even as he played with her breasts. Beneath her dress, her nipples bunched to points. When he drew back, she was definitely wide awake, and a flush of excitement pinkened her cheeks.

Nolan spotted the trainee and jerked his head. The young man headed over, his big brown eyes filled with desire to please. He started to kneel, and Nolan growled, freezing him in place. "Stand up, sub."

Austin rose and waited for instructions, a pulse beating fast in his throat.

"Bring me a screwdriver from the bar."

Austin started, "This one—"

Nolan gave him a cold look.

"Yes, Sir!" The young man left much faster than he'd arrived.

"You enjoy terrifying everyone around you?" Beth asked and stiffened. "I'm sorry, Sir."

"I'm just surrounded by timid people," he said, ignoring her apology. He rubbed his knuckles over her nipples. Her little breasts with correspondingly small nipples were more fun to play with than he'd thought. He'd gotten into a rut, taking only well-endowed women. He tugged on the knot at the top of her dress, pleased that the ties went from the neckline to the hem. With one hand, he undid the lacing she'd worked so patiently on earlier. He pulled the ties through the grommets, one by one, until her dress flapped open. Sliding his hand through the opening, he cupped a breast and felt the nipple gather even tighter.

Austin appeared with her drink, and Nolan set it into her hand with a nod of thanks for the sub. She frowned at the glass.

He gave her a steady gaze until she took a sip. He agreed with the Shadowland's two drink limit, but one drink wouldn't hurt her, and if anyone needed to mellow out, it would be this woman. He continued playing with her body, tracing the indentations of her ribs, circling her cute bellybutton, stroking the hollow above her collarbone. She sipped her drink so slowly that she'd started to squirm under his attentions before she finished.

Good. Her punishment would go easier if she was aroused, and punishment there would be. "Now, let's discuss what happened earlier."

Her eyes widened.

"Did you think I had forgotten?"

Her breath stopped.

"I believe we had an agreement, and you deliberately found someone else to top you. I am angry both about the broken agreement and, even more, that you didn't have the courtesy to speak to me first."

Her head dropped, her hands twining together on her lap. "You're right. What I did was rude."

"Why, sugar? Tell me why." Cupping her chin in his hand, he forced her to meet his gaze.

Beth didn't want to look at him, wanted to look anywhere but at him, but he didn't let her move. "I thought I'd be okay, that the block was gone."

"That doesn't explain why you wanted to change Doms."

"I was scared," she managed. "You scare me. I can't think when you touch me, and I have no control, and it's too much like what happened...before."

"You trusted him, and he betrayed you. Now you aren't sure if you can trust anyone."

That he could understand so well was a gift she didn't deserve.

His thumb stroked her cheek gently. "Little rabbit, I can understand your worries. And we, you and I, will work through them. But I cannot condone how you avoided talking to me."

He was going to hurt her. She knew it and didn't know if she could take it. He wouldn't be like the Dom earlier. The pain from being paddled had been intense, but this muscular man could do so, so much worse.

"I'll try to…" She felt her lips quiver, firmed them immediately, and closed her eyes so he wouldn't see the tears. Crying only made punishments worse.

"Look at me, sugar." She lifted her eyes, and he wiped away the tear that spilled over. "I could tell you what I do and don't do, but you wouldn't believe a word I said. So let's get this over with." Still sitting, he pushed her to her feet. "Strip."

She glanced at the spanking station and saw a Dom fastening his sub onto the bench. "But someone is already—"

"The only words that leave your mouth are, 'Yes, Sir.' Am I clear?"

"Yes, Sir." She'd never stripped in the bar itself, only in a scene area. This felt all wrong. Totally humiliating even if the eyes on her were the same ones that would watch a scene. But it was playacting there, not real. Out here was real.

Master Nolan didn't speak. Only his fingers tapping the arm of the couch showed that his patience might be limited.

She pressed her lips together to keep from saying anything and peeled off her dress, pathetically glad she hadn't worn underwear. And there she stood, naked except for the thin black cuffs around her wrists.

His eyes ran up and down her body, and her breasts pebbled under his warm gaze. How could he rouse her with a look when others couldn't with hands and mouths and cocks?

"You have a nice little body," he said after far too long a pause. He rose and held out his hand. "Come then."

Adding to her confusion, he led her away from the stations along the wall. At the end of the long oval bar, he stopped. "Cullen, I have a decoration for your bar. And can you spare a towel?"

The bartender barked out a laugh and tossed him a clean towel. "The scenery here has been boring. Go ahead."

Bar decoration? Beth's eyes widened, and her stomach clenched. She took a step back. *He wouldn't.*

Flipping the towel open on the bar top, Master Nolan picked her up and set her on the bar.

"Sir. No, this—"

He shot her a cold look, and she bit back further protests, although more and more welled up inside her as she became aware of people watching, of their grins and murmured comments. Her cheeks flushed hot.

Sir stepped back and considered her for a moment. "Close, but not quite right. I've always liked the silhouettes on truckers' mud flaps. Lean back onto your hands." Setting a hand between her breasts, he pushed her back until her weight was on her arms.

Her breasts jutted upward, and he ran a hand over them. A jolt, then embarrassment ran through her at his casual touch. He treated her like a toy.

"Nolan, I prefer that my decorations face *me*," Cullen yelled from down the bar.

Sir grunted. "Well, that's reasonable. I wouldn't want to annoy the bartender." Lifting her slightly, he spun her around. Now her legs, rather than dangling off the end of the bar, lay on the bar top. He bent her knees and set her feet widely apart, exposing her pussy to every person sitting at the bar. She closed her eyes, and a tremor ran through her. She'd almost, almost rather have been whipped.

Master Raoul walked by, slowing to look at her, then Nolan. "I don't suppose you're serving appetizers, are you?"

"Sorry. I missed supper, so I'm going to keep this little dish for myself."

Beth sighed in relief, then choked when Sir lowered his head to suck on the breast closest to him. She started to sit up, and he turned his head, just enough to look at her, his lips an inch from her breast, his breath warm on her wet nipple. "Do not move at all. Not one inch."

Her fingers curled as she stilled. She kept her body stiff and unmoving as he licked her nipple and circled it with his tongue. Each stroke of his wet tongue sent sensation scorching through her, and moisture trickled down the folds of her pussy. Oh, God.

"Need your second beer, Nolan?" Cullen called as he concocted a drink.

Sir lifted his head. "That would go down well." He turned and leaned against the bar, his elbow resting lightly on her hip. Almost carelessly, he stroked her inner thigh as he started talking to the man next to him.

The man said he was a fairly new club member… He'd joined with his wife… Beth lost track of the conversation as Sir's warm hand moved over her leg, her waist, fingering the tender crease where her thigh met her hip.

Despite being naked, she felt as if heat waves were rising from her skin. When Sir laid his hand on the inside of her thigh and brushed his knuckles against the curls of her pussy, all Beth could do was close her eyes. *Don't move. Don't move.*

"Well, it was nice meeting you, Nolan."

Beth opened her eyes to see the man shake hands with Sir. The man glanced at Beth and the position of Sir's hand. His face colored slightly before he hurried off.

Beth knew her face was probably just as red. Sir glanced back at her, his eyes crinkling. His fingers brushed against the swollen lips of her pussy, yanking her attention to his touch as if he'd pulled her on a leash. As his knuckles trailed back and forth, he watched her struggles to stay still, to breathe normally.

Cullen arrived with Sir's beer. "Here you go, Nolan. Sorry about the wait."

"No problem." Sir took the beer from Cullen and then looked at Beth. His lips curved into the faintest of smiles, and she tensed. What was he—

He splashed some beer onto her breasts. She jerked as the icy liquid hit. Her nipples tightened into hard buds.

Arms resting on the bar, Master Nolan slowly licked the drops away, laving her nipples until she almost whimpered. His tongue followed the trail of cold beer to where it pooled in her belly button. He lapped it up like a dog. After a minute, he returned to lick one nipple lightly, then he bit down gently, repeating it over and over until fire shot from her breast to her clit, until she had to lock her teeth over a moan. Then he switched to the other breast.

"Nolan, I've been hoping you'd be here."

Sir straightened as a hefty Domme in biker clothes walked over. A short, voluptuous sub in a tight latex dress with breast and pussy cutouts trailed behind her

"Good to see you, Olivia." As he turned to talk with the woman, his big hand closed firmly over Beth's ankle. The Domme gave Beth an amused look, then ignored her as she asked Sir about remodeling her house to add a dungeon room.

All Sir's attention appeared to be on Olivia, except his hand kept inching higher up Beth's leg. His fingers traced little circles on her inner thigh, spiraling ever higher until he touched her pussy. Even then, he never looked at her, just moved enough to rest his forearm on her lower stomach. His fingers dangled right over her pussy. His dark bronze arm was a startling contrast to her pale skin, his hand so wide it covered her mound completely.

"How close are your neighbors?" he asked the Domme, even as his fingers curled, stroking through Beth's betrayingly wet folds. Slowly, unpredictably, his fingers caressed her opening, then spread the dampness over her clit. Sensation sizzled through her nerves. Her folds and clit swelled, feeling too tight as if the skin couldn't contain the blood rushing to the area.

He touched her clit again, rubbed briefly, and then dipped into her opening.

Her breath strangled in her throat. She tried to ignore what he was doing, tried to stop the need rising within her. Dammit, why now? Any other Dom and she'd have been fine, not even slightly aroused.

This Dom… He didn't seem to care about her response, wasn't even looking at her. His wet finger traced over the sensitive edge between her clit and its hood, stroking it, over and over. Pressure built within her, the exquisite sensations bringing her almost to the peak. Almost. His conversation with the Domme buzzed in her ears, only the slide of his fingers was real. If he'd just touch her… She bit her lips. Her hips tilted only the slightest amount.

He slapped her thigh. The sharp sting stabbed through her like an electric current. "Stay still, sub."

The Domme laughed, thanked him for his advice, and strolled away. Her sub gave Beth a sympathetic look before following.

Sir turned, his dark eyes cool as his gaze ran over Beth. She held perfectly still, tried to control her breathing, pleading with her eyes, *Let me down, let me down.*

He took a sip of his beer, another, started to set the bottle down, and stopped. He studied her again…and then he poured his cold beer right onto her overheated, sensitive clit. She gasped audibly, her legs jerking upward.

"Don't move, sub." She received another stinging slap onto her thigh that somehow only increased her need.

Her whole body was shaking now, her clit throbbing with need. Yet she was horrified when he lifted the leg closest to him and set her ankle onto his shoulder. He wouldn't… *No, no, no!*

He scooted her hips toward him, bent, and started lapping the beer from her pussy. The first stroke of his tongue sent a blaze streaking through her; the next touch coiled the tension inside her higher. She heard her fingernails scratching the bar top. She tried to stay still and not move as his tongue circled her clit, the hood, the side, wiggling underneath, the other side, around and around. The tissue grew so engorged, so sensitive that every slide stopped her breath, shooting her closer and closer. The room faded. All she could feel was his tongue stroking over her, his unyielding grip on her leg.

Suddenly he thrust a rough finger into her, hard and fast, the invasion shocking. Overwhelming. Everything stretched and burst at once, exploding outward in waves of pleasure. She bucked against his face, her insides spasming around the thrusting finger. Somehow she managed to smother her scream so only muffled cries escaped.

Her arms shook, almost giving out. Master Nolan lifted his head, amusement flickering in his black eyes as he looked at her. He replaced her foot on the bar and adjusted her legs to the previous position. He patted her thigh, ignored her labored breathing, and said, "Don't move, pet."

Cullen walked over, shaking his head. "You know, if you didn't want to drink from the bottle, I would have brought you a glass."

Sir chuckled. "I like my way better." He rested his forearm back on her stomach, his fingers trailing down against her pussy, and she barely suppressed a moan. *Not again, please, not again.*

Petal-soft touches danced over her clit, and her body sprang back to awareness.

"You know only a barbarian would refuse to use a glass." The bartender glanced over Sir's shoulder and grinned. "Like my new bar ornament, Z?"

Oh, dear sweet God. Beth stiffened, her humiliation complete as Master Z walked around Sir.

He turned and looked at her, his silver gaze mildly interested. "Very pretty, Cullen." Looking at Sir with a faint smile, he lifted a brow. "I do believe I provide several well-equipped stations for scenes."

Master Nolan patted her mound, making her jump. "I would never do a scene at the bar, Z. This was punishment."

"Indeed." Master Z tilted his head. "Did I not hear scenelike noises coming from this area?"

"Well, you know how I hate to drink from the bottle." From the side, she could see Sir's eyes crinkle. His finger started stroking through her wetness, relentlessly rubbing against her clit. As the inescapable pleasure surged through her, the muscles in her legs tensed, quivering uncontrollably as she strove not to move.

Sir continued. "Cullen didn't give me a glass so I used what was available."

"Don't be blaming me, you bastard," Cullen said.

"Well, that explains it." Eyes lit with laughter, Master Z glanced at Beth, at where Sir's hand lay, and he coughed. Another surge of heat ran through Beth, this time from pure embarrassment. "I do approve of punishment though. And I've noticed the submissives in the club are becoming extremely uppity."

Cullen tapped his fingers on the bar. "That's a serious problem. Are you planning a solution?"

"I am." Z smiled slowly. "Some sales reps have been after me to let them demo their equipment. I've decided to have a machine day."

Machine? Beth tried to ignore the insistent movement of Nolan's fingers. What kind of machines would a BDSM club use? Winches?

"Machines?" Cullen asked. "You lost me."

"Fucking machines, Cullen." Master Z's gaze drifted over Beth. "I intend, by the end of that evening, there won't be a sub able to walk."

Cullen barked a laugh.

Nolan chuckled, turning to run an assessing gaze over Beth, one that made her stomach knot. "Now that might be fun. I think she likes objects being inserted here and there." His finger slid into her, and she gasped, her senses flaring.

"Switching to another subject," Z said. "I plan to remodel upstairs and add another office, perhaps change the kitchen. Can you come by sometime and give me an estimate?"

"How about Tuesday? Maybe around four or so?"

"That will work well."

As Master Z strolled away, Sir glanced at Cullen. "All that talking left me dry." He picked up the beer bottle, and Beth could hear the swish of remaining liquid. He smiled at her.

Not again. Losing control on top of the bar, having no… "Please, Sir," she whispered, and her voice trembled. "No. Please, Master."

His eyebrows lifted. "Would you prefer to do this elsewhere? Upstairs?"

The private rooms. Alone with a Dom who could do anything. The rooms might not be monitored. Her stomach twisted.

"Not yet, I see." Sir contemplated her for a minute, his fingers tapping her clit, never letting the excitement die. "You know, there *is* another bed in this place."

She frowned, trying to think of where he meant.

"Hand me my toy bag, would you, Cullen?"

The bartender pulled a black bag from the shelves under the bar. "Sure you wouldn't rather stay here? She sure is a pretty decoration."

"I have a feeling she'll be back someday." After slinging the bag over his right shoulder, Sir plucked Beth off the bar and threw her over his other shoulder. She let out a startled yip, appalled to find herself head down, secured by his hands on her bare thighs.

A chorus of complaints came from the people around the bar.

"Hey, put her back."

"Cullen, don't let him walk away with your ornament."

"It was just getting interesting."

Her head spun as Sir carried her through the room. Just as she began to get her bearings, she felt one of his hands edge between her legs and rub against her pussy lips. Incredulity filled her as he walked through the crowd, her ass in the air and his fingers in her crotch. She wiggled, kicked a little. Maybe he'd put her down—at least he'd have to move his hand.

He turned his head and nipped her thigh, the sharp pain streaking straight to her clit. "Stay still," he growled.

Chapter Six

When his little sub froze on his shoulder, Nolan smiled and slid his finger another inch into the tightness between her legs. She squirmed again, this time uncontrollably. The tantalizing scent of her arousal mingled with her light fragrance of strawberries. He nodded at the club members he knew and smiled at Mistress Anne who was followed by her sweat-streaked, exhausted…glowing…sub.

At the back of the club, he went down the long hallway. The windows on the right showed the medical room where some lucky male sub was getting an enema. Then the dungeon. Nolan turned left and into the playroom.

The flickering sconces in the playroom illumined dark red walls covered with fancy ironwork. A very, very big bed covered with black satin filled the entire room leaving only two feet of walking room around the edges. Ropes and chains with cuffs were attached to the bed frame sides and dangled from the iron headboard and footboard. The dark music of Depeche Mode drowned out the sounds of the club. Two other couples were using the room and had apparently migrated together to make one happy foursome.

Nolan chose an empty corner near the head of the bed and dropped the little rabbit onto her back.

She sat up, looked around, and realized where they were. Some of the worry faded from her eyes, but the confusion remained. Apparently he'd found another place she hadn't used before. Good enough.

"Wrists, please," he said, holding his hand out. She set her wrists in them without a pause, a well-trained sub. He flattened her on her back and secured her cuffs to the headboard. Resting a hip on the bed, he enjoyed the sight of her in the dim light of the room. Big turquoise eyes. Red hair spilling out over the black satin cover. Her breasts had no sag, sitting up nicely on her rib cage. He slowly ran a hand over her erect nipples, watched them peak. Her arms and legs were slender, but muscles rippled under the soft female padding. Her ribs showed, her stomach concave with no fat there at all. She could use a few more pounds on her.

The hair of her pussy glinted a pretty red-brown that matched the freckles over her shoulders and cheeks. Of course, he preferred bare…something he'd deal with at a later time.

"What are you doing?" she asked, her nervousness overcoming her discipline.

He smiled. A sub shouldn't be terrified, but a little anxiety was good. He ran a finger between her pretty breasts down the center of her stomach. "Just enjoying the view, sugar. I like to look at you."

She blushed, the compliment confusing her more than anything he'd done yet.

He leaned down and pleased himself by taking her lips, easing into a demanding kiss. She tasted of orange juice with her own sweetness underneath. He pulled back and ran his finger over her wet lips. "I intend to put that mouth to a different use one of these days. Will that be a problem?"

She had just enough time to shake her head before he held her head between his hands and captured her mouth again. The little quiver, the slight arch of her body said she liked being secured and overpowered.

And he enjoyed the hell out of doing it. He moved down her body, spent some time bringing her nipples to a darker color, sucking the velvety tips until they peaked long and narrow. Until the scent of her arousal surrounded her body.

"Spread your legs for me." He waited until she complied, her eyes holding just a touch of fear now. Right on the edge of fear was where trust could grow. Since the gentle path of time and communication—and *nice* Doms—hadn't worked for her, he'd take her to the mountains instead.

He studied her and then smiled. How many times could he get her off before her eyes would lose the wariness and look only dazed? *Be worth the effort to find out.* So he settled himself between her thighs and licked upward through the center of her folds and right over her clit. Her stomach muscles clenched, and he heard the sharp intake of breath. She'd probably come to expect slow from him. *Time to learn different.*

With firm fingers, he spread her pussy lips open, exposed her glistening clit, and sucked it into his mouth. Her cry rang through the room, and he could see her hands grasp the iron bars of the headboard. *Smart girl. Hang on tight.* His tongue rubbed her clit, up and down, stroking relentlessly, first one side, then the other, and as it emerged from the hood, he licked right over the top. She came immediately, still muffling her cries, her hips trying to bounce despite his forearms pressing her flat.

No screaming? She wasn't losing it yet, then. He slid up her body, covering her, enjoying the feel of her breasts against his chest. She felt so delicate with little hipbones poking him and a prominent collarbone to slide his tongue over. She blinked at him, and he saw awareness return a little too quickly. Yes, he definitely had work to do yet.

"Thank you, Sir," she whispered.

She probably didn't realize how much he enjoyed eating pussy. Many Doms didn't. More fools them. A woman was never more vulnerable than when bound with her legs spread wide and a tongue on her clit. "We'll see if you still thank me when I'm done."

As her brows drew together, he snatched another kiss before returning to his labors. He added some finger-fucking. She had a nice snug little sheath and an easily accessible G-spot. When she arched up this time, a high cry escaped her. Not quite a scream, but not bad. When he lay back over her, her breathing sounded ragged, and her heart rate had definitely increased.

"Thank you," she said, looking unsure whether he should be thanked. Three orgasms in a fifteen-minute period didn't seem like much to him, but she'd had a long dry spell there. "What about you, Sir?"

The question, despite her obvious shrinking away, warmed his heart, and he ran a finger over her soft cheek. "You're right, little rabbit; it's my turn." Remembering the Dom who'd taken her earlier, he added, "I don't think I'll need any lube, do you?"

She flushed.

Beth prepared herself mentally as Sir rolled off her to kneel beside his toy bag. She didn't mind being taken, not really, although it didn't do anything for her, and made her feel…used…sometimes, like just a—

He stripped off his shirt, and her mind blanked. His chest seemed bigger as the shadowy light flickered over strong pectorals and ridged abdominal muscles. With easy movements, he undid his leathers and sheathed himself in a condom. He took something from his bag. Picking up her feet, he slid it up her legs. She lifted her head. It looked almost like a thong with a tiny rubber triangle. He adjusted the soft piece until it lay right on top of her clit. Her very sensitive clit.

"What's that?"

"You've never played with a butterfly before?" The sun lines at the corners of his eyes crinkled. "We'll discuss your impressions later tonight." After dropping a tiny device beside her head, he settled on top of her, kneeing her legs apart. The bare skin of his chest felt searingly hot against her breasts. His thick erection pressed against her pussy, and he reached down to swirl it in her wetness. When he picked up the little device and something clicked, she realized it was a remote control.

The butterfly thing hummed, vibrating gently on her clit. She stiffened at the feel of it, her mouth dropping open when her body began to rouse in spite of how many times she'd come.

He smiled, his eyes hungry. He bent his head and sucked a nipple into his mouth, nipping hard enough to have her jerk, hard enough to send zinging sensations through her body to join the seething tension pooling in her lower half from the…thing.

Her hips rocked up and down as she approached another climax. Her vagina involuntarily tightened, and her legs, pressed widely open by his body, trembled.

"I think you're ready, now, don't you?" he murmured. With one hand, he positioned himself and thrust into her, deep and fast.

Every nerve in her body short-circuited all at once. "Aaah!" Electricity shot from her pussy through her, searing all the way to her toes and fingertips. Her vagina convulsed around his cock.

"There's a good girl," he murmured and took her mouth for a deep kiss. When he drew back, he braced himself on his forearms and looked in her eyes, then smiled slightly at whatever he'd seen.

She sure didn't know. She felt confused, like she'd fallen into a different world, one filled with heat and sensation and light. Stunned, she realized the vibrations over her clit had stopped.

Her breathing slowed eventually, and her heart stopped hammering on the inside of her ribs. After a minute, she frowned. *He hadn't come…* "Sir, you—"

He grinned at her, the amusement in his eyes as obvious as his enjoyment of her. And then he moved, pushing his cock deeper into her, and she realized he'd barely entered her before. Oh, God, he was much, much bigger than she was used to. She began to feel overstretched, filled unbearably full. She yanked at her hands, wanting to push him away, but he continued relentlessly, his black gaze focused on her eyes, her face.

Finally he stopped, and she could feel his balls pressing against her. His cock was so thick in her that she could barely breathe.

"Am I hurting you?" he asked. As if he didn't know.

"Yes." But her body had begun to adjust, the devastating sense of invasion subsiding. "No. No, Sir."

"Honest sub." His eyes warmed with approval in a way that made her feel…good. Valued.

As her body relaxed, her hands unfisted, and she drew a deeper breath.

"There we go." His lips curved. He moved inside her, and she gasped at the overwhelming feeling. He slid out slowly, pressed back in, and continued, increasing his speed by fractions.

There was no pain now. She didn't feel all that involved, but tried to cooperate, tightening her muscles, moving her hips.

He chuckled and captured her mouth in a hot, wet kiss. "Sex is a team sport, sugar." Reaching over her head, he hit the remote, and the butterfly thing hummed right over her clit. The vibrations were faster and stronger this time. He moved inside her relentlessly now, each thrust slamming the thing into her.

As the intense vibrations pulsed into her clit, her insides flared to life as if a fire had been sparked. Her pussy contracted as each stroke sent her higher. Her clit throbbed, the slide of his cock wakening more nerves with each long glide. Her hips pressed up trying to get more.

When he slowed, she whimpered.

The vibrations stopped, but somehow her clit seemed to have absorbed them, leaving her body strung taut, right on the edge. "Please, Sir." She pushed her hips up.

He lowered his weight, keeping her immobile. Balancing on his elbows, he set his big hands on each side of her face, forcing her to look into his dangerous eyes. "Do you like having me inside you, Beth?" He moved just enough to send shudders through her.

"Yes, Sir."

"Do you trust me, Beth?"

"I—" His eyes… She couldn't lie when he looked at her like that, when he surrounded her, inside, outside. "I—"

"All right then, I want you to say the words whether you believe them or not." He moved inside her slowly, keeping her so close to the edge that her body couldn't relax. His rough voice deepened. "'I trust you, Master Nolan. You will keep me safe.' Say that."

She hesitated, and he stopped moving. Oh, God. "I trust you, Master Nolan. You will keep me safe." But she didn't trust him; she didn't trust anyone.

He slid out. In. The sensation so intense her body tried to arch against him. He held her in place. "Again."

"God, please…" she pleaded, met only implacable black eyes, and pushed the words out, "I trust you, Master Nolan. You will keep me safe."

He gave her two slow strokes and stopped. Waited.

"I trust you, Master Nolan. You will keep me safe." She hurried the words, needing more.

Three strokes, each one searing down her nerve paths, sparks flaring from the contact. Stopped.

Whimpers mingled with the words. "I trust you, Master Nolan. You will keep me safe." A breath. "I trust you, Master Nolan. You will keep me safe."

The words turned into a chant, burning into her brain as he started stroking again with hard, sure thrusts.

"I trust you, Master Nolan. You will keep me safe." His eyes held hers transfixed, and she felt something inside her soul shiver and crack. Tears ran down her cheeks. "I trust you, Master Nolan. You will keep me safe." The words took on an urgency, a reality as he melded their bodies together, as her muscles strained against his.

And then the vibrations over her clit started again even as he sped up. The sensations rolled through her like an unstoppable earthquake, and her world burst apart with a shattering orgasm. Her eyes went blind as her insides convulsed, billowing around the thick, intruding cock, setting off more and more spasms. She could hear herself screaming.

When her shudders slowed, he started to thrust again, and she arched up into him with another cry. His cock seemed to swell as he hammered into her with short, fast strokes. He gave a guttural groan, and she felt his cock jerk inside her, each movement making her pussy clench.

"Oh, God," she whispered. Her mind had gone out of focus. Her heart beat so forcefully it should have knocked him off of her.

He chuckled. "No need to go that far. 'Oh, Master' will do."

She was too far gone to do more than frown at him.

He chuckled again and nibbled her neck as he reached up to undo her cuffs, then rolled, still seated firmly inside her twitching vagina, and settled her firmly on top of him. His hand pressed her head down into the hollow of his shoulder. "Shhh, sugar. Time to relax."

Her arms hurt as she moved to grasp his wide shoulders. Her fingers dug in, as though, if she could hang onto him firmly enough, her world would stop spinning. His muscles flexed under her hands. She couldn't seem to think, but it didn't matter. She knew she'd normally be trembling right now, except she was too exhausted, too limp. The sounds of the others coupling and talking in the room seemed distant. Unimportant.

Licking her dry lips, she tried to speak, not knowing what to say. The chant echoed in her head, diminishing slowly until only one word remained. *Safe, safe, safe.*

His hand moved over her back, warm against the cooling sweat covering her body. He massaged her tender bottom, pressing her hips against him and chuckling when her vagina spasmed weakly. The fragrance of sex surrounded her, mingling with Sir's soapy, musky scent and her own.

His voice rumbled, low and a little husky. The sound of a satisfied man. The sound of Sir. "I enjoyed that very much, Beth."

The open pleasure sent a glow through her. How long had it been since a Dom had been happy with her? She snuggled closer.

"I like your body," he murmured, his hand cupping her bottom. "I like all those muscles you have. Your fiery hair. Your freckles."

She hated her freckles. "I always wanted skin the color of yours." She ran her hand over his chest, enjoying the feel of satiny skin stretched over his contoured curves. "I like your muscles too."

"You're not worried about my strength being used against you?"

The question shot fear through her, and she knew he felt her stiffen. His hand stroked her hair.

"Beth, answer me."

She pressed her forehead to his chest, inhaled his warmth. "Sometimes. Yes."

"Thank you for being honest." He lifted her up enough to look into her eyes. "The one thing I insist upon is honesty. Don't ever lie to me." The roughness of his voice rubbed over her senses like gravel in an open wound, and she shivered.

Could not admitting something be considered a lie?

Chapter Seven

Early Monday evening, Nolan pulled up in front of the Shadowlands and parked his truck behind Beth's gardening trailer. The humid air wrapped around him as he walked over to lean against her truck and wait for her. Was she going to be pleased to see him or terrified?

He rarely dated women he met at the club, but last Saturday had revealed unexpected facets of her personality, and he'd decided to make an exception in her case. Her courage in admitting her mistake had gained his respect. The contrast between her sexual hunger and her deep fears yanked at his Dom nature. And the amazement on her face each time she climaxed… What man could resist that?

So far, everything between them had been about domination and sex. The chemistry was there, both sexual and Dom/sub, but he'd seen an expression on her face a few times that hinted she wanted more.

He edged over into a patch of shade and pulled out his PDA. Might as well get a little work done while he waited.

"Hey."

Nolan looked up, glanced at the sun, and realized at least half an hour had gone by. "There you are. I've been waiting for you."

Beth wore an off-white tank top and khaki shorts, and the sight of her in street clothes was as big a turn-on as her club clothes. Her cheeks had a pretty flush, and her red hair was tangled. A trickle of sweat ran down between her breasts, and the thought of pinning her against the truck and licking it off made him harden. But no, this wasn't about sex today.

"Why didn't you come and find me?"

He shrugged. "I don't like interruptions when I'm working; figured you wouldn't either."

"Oh. Um, thank you. And you're waiting for me because..."

As he moved closer, she retreated until halted by her truck, her back against the door. Nolan braced an arm on each side of her head, trapping her. With pleasure, he noticed that the little rabbit didn't look nearly as terrified today. More progress. He rewarded himself with a kiss, soft and wet and hot, only his mouth touching, since if his hands landed on her, he'd probably take her right there against the truck.

Drawing back, he smiled at her dazed eyes and wet lips and said, "Aside from needing to do that, I thought I would take you out for supper."

"Supper?" Her hands were on his chest, and she snatched them off as if she'd committed some crime.

"Beth, I like your hands on me," he said. "Put them back." He waited until her delicate fingers curled over his shoulders. He recalled how pretty her wrists looked in cuffs, how she pulled at the restraints while he... *Hell.*

He cleared his throat. "Supper. You have to eat—and eat more than you've been doing, I might add—and I'm hungry. There's an Italian place just down the road, one where we won't look too out of place in work clothes."

"Food." Her mind was obviously not on that kind of hunger. The way she looked at his mouth then away, her hands stroking his muscles, the dilation of her pupils... She wanted him whether she knew it or not. His temperature shot up at least ten degrees. Just how fast would she run if he took her up on that unconscious invitation?

But he didn't want her running; she was just beginning to trust him. A little.

"Yes, food." He squeezed the nape of her neck. "You aren't ready to be alone with me, so we're going to go have supper. Now." Before he ripped off her shorts and buried himself inside her so deep and hard that she wouldn't walk for a week.

As if she could hear him, her blue-green eyes widened, and she swallowed. "All right." Her voice came out husky, reminding him of how it sounded after she'd come.

He moved her away from her truck, pushed her in front of him, and swatted her trim little ass to keep her moving. "Good. My truck is over there."

* * *

As they were led to a table at the Italian place, Beth noticed the enthusiastic greetings Nolan received from several waitresses. He obviously came here often, and no woman would easily forget him.

He held Beth's chair, then took a seat across from her. She could see what the waitresses saw. A formidable man. His blue work shirt didn't disguise the powerful muscles underneath, and the top buttons were open revealing his corded neck. The man simply radiated force, his bearing supremely self-confident. Many of the Doms changed when outside of the scene, away from their club. Not him. This was not a good old boy, but a forceful, dangerous man.

Her heart missed a beat when his gaze met hers. He smiled slowly. "Relax, sugar, there's no bar top here to decorate."

She flushed from her toes to her face. Was this what a hot flash would feel like in twenty years? *God.*

The waitress handed them menus, managing to touch Sir's hand as she did. Beth's teeth clamped together as unexpected jealousy snapped through her like a rubber band.

They ordered. He frowned and added a side dish to hers. As the waitress bustled away, he leaned back and studied Beth. "I know you run a yard service. What kind of work does that entail?"

She looked into his face, amazed to see real interest. Oh, he really shouldn't leave himself open that way. She launched into a description of maintenance, of weeding and mowing and trimming, of planning and design. Rather than looking bored, he asked another question. And another. Their salads came, and she dug in, actually hungry for a change.

"Where did you learn all that? From college?" he asked.

"No, my father ran a nursery with a landscaping service, and I'd help around the place and go out with the men.

Someday I want to start my own nursery." She confessed her dream before thinking, and then tensed, expecting him to sneer.

His eyes narrowed, but he answered easily, "Sounds like you'd be good at it. Jessica could probably help you with planning how to finance it and the paperwork. She knows all the ins and outs of small business accounting."

Something relaxed inside her. He hadn't laughed. Had even suggested…Jessica? Beth shook her head in surprise. Why hadn't she thought about asking Jessica for help?

She felt a tremor of excitement as her dream began to leaf out. "That's a great idea. Thank you."

She worked on her salad, nibbled a pepper, and studied him in turn. An uneasy feeling ran through her. This man had been inside her, had done incredibly intimate things to her, and she didn't know him at all. Her face warmed as she cleared her throat. "What about you? What do you do?"

He'd already finished his salad. He pushed the plate off to one side and refilled their wine glasses. "I'm a contractor. Construction."

No wonder he was so muscular. Her lips pursed. "The housing market's dead. Are you doing all right?"

"I do mostly office buildings, and Tampa is growing nicely, despite the economy." He grinned at her. "Like you, I followed in my father's footsteps. He owns a construction company back in Texas."

"I wondered where your accent came from. Why aren't you still in Texas?"

"My wife had family back here, and she didn't want to live too far from them. She talked me into moving here."

The unexpected blow took her breath away. "You're married?"

"No, sugar. I wouldn't be playing in the club if I was married. I got a divorce about seven years ago. My wife cheated on me, and that was it." His gaze landed on her, straight and level. "I despise liars, and I figure cheating is just another way of lying."

This blow was almost worse. Her eyes dropped to her left hand where the white line from her wedding ring had slowly faded over the past year.

Their main course came, the lasagna bubbling in the stoneware dish, and yet the scent of the spicy sauce turned her stomach now. *Cheating. Lying.*

Had her husband cheated on her? Nolan watched the little sub's face. All the animation had faded, and the sparkle in her blue-green eyes had dimmed. Her appetite had disappeared as well. Dammit. Some women ate when unhappy or stressed; Beth was obviously not one of them. He felt like pulling her onto his lap and telling her everything would be all right.

He'd enjoyed listening to her talk. Obviously competent at her job, overflowing with enthusiasm, her energy unleashed. A far cry from the wary little rabbit in the club. Seeing the difference in her increased his determination to help her heal… And maybe someday she'd bring all that enthusiasm to making love.

"I have a house in the country. A few acres on a small lake," he said, toying with a piece of garlic bread. "The view is really pretty, but the entire acreage is weeds and stubble. I could use a designer..."

She lit up as if he'd handed her a dozen roses. "I'd love to give you some ideas. Maybe—"

He could see the moment she realized she'd have to visit his house. Be alone with him. *Little rabbit.* He gave an exasperated sigh. "Would you be interested if I arrange something so you won't be alone with me?"

"I'm sorry, Sir."

"Nolan, sugar." He took her hand and rubbed her thin fingers, knowing now where the calluses had come from. "I answer to Nolan outside of the club."

"So you don't do the full master-slave routine?" Her fingers trembled for an instant.

"Take a bite and I'll tell you." He waited until she started on her untouched lasagna. "I had a slave for almost a year, but I uncollared her before I left for Iraq."

Her fork stopped halfway to her mouth. He frowned at her until the bite disappeared. Her eyes were filled with questions she was too timid to ask.

"No, I'm not involved with anyone now. No, I don't want a slave again."

Relief, plain and simple, showed on her face, then confusion. "But why not? I thought all men liked that."

"Some do. Maybe less than you'd think, at least after trying it." He nodded at her food again and grinned when she rolled her eyes before taking a bite.

"Think about it, sugar. You're not only responsible for your own well-being, but for someone else's also. Making day-to-day decisions for them, all the time, without a break." He lifted her fingers to his mouth, kissed them. "Now, I will never give up control in the bedroom and I occasionally enjoy control at other times...like making you wear the butterfly when taking you to a restaurant." He gave her a wicked smile and could almost see the erotic images float into her head. When he nipped her finger, she flushed a gorgeous red.

"But the rest of the time, I'd prefer to have a partner, not a slave. Does that make sense?"

"Ah. Yes." She was still pink.

He grinned and throttled it down. No sex today, whether she wanted it or not. *Dammit.*

* * *

Kyler glanced at his wristwatch and scowled. Almost 2:00 p.m. He couldn't afford to wait any longer or he'd miss his plane.

Hell. Nothing was working out as it should.

Fury surged through him as he looked around the hovel Elizabeth lived in—a fucking studio apartment with cheap furniture. The place didn't even have a real bedroom. The bitch actually preferred living in poverty to being with him. Well, she wouldn't be here for long, would she?

Walking around the room, he tossed a few items into a grocery sack: a CD player and CDs, loose cash, the few pieces of jewelry from the dresser. He took enough that she'd believe a burglar had broken in.

He glanced at the door and smiled at the memory of the wood shattering. Not as satisfying as breaking bones, of course, but that time would come. Soon. Perhaps he should thank her for choosing an apartment in the back of the complex.

If only he had time to deal with her now. But her punishment would take a while, and he had to be in court early tomorrow, Wednesday. After that, if he worked late and put in some time on the holiday, his partners could manage to cover his cases for a few days.

He tucked his notepad into a pocket. He'd gone through her files, taken down information from her bills and address book. Even if she managed to escape him now, he'd find her again quickly.

And once he finished with her this time, she would not be capable of running again.

* * *

Beth unlocked the gate in the eight-foot fence at the back of the Shadowlands and entered Z's private gardens. Thunder rumbled overhead, and along the fence line, purple fountain grass rustled in the stiffening breeze. She was running late, but just had to pause and enjoy the sight before her.

Over the past couple of months, she'd worked on changing the appearance of the huge yard. The previously formal landscaping was evolving into casual, even a bit wild.

With a contractor's help, she'd given the swimming pool area the appearance of a tropical pond where water gurgled through a faux rocky stream to splash into the clear-blue pool.

Wildly flowering gardens carved the big yard into smaller garden rooms, each with a theme. To the right, a Jacuzzi room. Closer to the house with a view of the rising sun, the breakfast nook held a small table and wrought iron chairs. In the contemplation room near the back, she'd planted soothing blue flowers.

Now looking at her work, she felt pride rising in her. She'd never had so much fun and look what she had wrought in such a short time. Lovely, lovely, lovely, if she said so herself.

"You going to stand there and admire your work all day?"

With a small scream, Beth jumped. The voice had come from above… Scowling, she looked up to see Jessica leaning over the third-story balcony.

"Next time," Beth said, "just shoot me instead of giving me a heart attack."

"Sorry." In shorts and a pale green tank top, Jessica trotted down the steps. "I saw you from the kitchen. C'mere, I've got a peace offering." As Beth entered the covered, screened lanai, the blonde handed over an ice-cold Coke. "Take a break for a minute."

"I had one already. That's why I'm running late." Beth opened the can and took a big gulp. "I swung by my apartment to grab something to eat and found someone had kicked my door in."

"Jeez, are you serious?"

"Smashed the frame and everything." And terrified her so badly she'd almost abandoned all she'd built and fled. But the couple next door had seen her and came running over. They walked into her apartment with her. A few things had been pilfered…her CD player and music, some jewelry. Just a burglary, and how weird was that to be relieved a burglar had been in her place?

After calming down, she had realized Kyler couldn't know where she was, and if he did, he'd do worse than just kick in her door. "At least I didn't have much to steal. The poor burglar was probably really disappointed."

"That's still scary. Is the door fixed?"

Beth felt anxiety curl in her stomach. "No. The maintenance guy broke his leg last week, so the manager's going nuts with complaints. Said she couldn't get anyone over to repair it till tomorrow. So after I finish setting the plants out, I'm going to fix what I can. And I'll put a chair under the knob tonight."

"I don't like the sound of that."

"Best I can do. But that's why I'm late getting here, and why I don't have time for a break." She glanced around casually. After remembering Nolan's arrangement with Z, she'd planned to come early and leave before he arrived. And now she was late, and his truck sat in the parking lot. Knowing he was upstairs made her feel weird. Itchy. She'd enjoyed being with him yesterday a little too much, at least until he talked about adultery. And lying.

Now she knew; she couldn't afford to get involved with him. She would have to keep their interactions casual and only for sex. At the club.

"It looks like you get a break whether you want one or not," Jessica said as the first drops of rain splattered on the wide leaves of the nearby pagoda plant. The blonde dropped into a chair at the wrought-iron-and-oak table and shoved a chair out for Beth. "Might as well sit till the storm passes."

"Oh, honestly." Thunder boomed overhead, and the rain increased, fat drops splashing on the grass like little explosions. Beth took the chair. "Are you always this persistent?"

Jessica laughed. "This is nothing. You should see me when it comes to travel expenses or office supply receipts. I can be a real bitch. Speaking of which, Nolan said you might want help figuring out how to open a nursery."

Beth felt her breath stop as her heart bobbed in her chest like a top-heavy flower. Nolan believed in her, believed she could do this. Could she? *Yes. Yes she could.* She put her hand over her jittery heart and jumped into the future. "I would. You mean you'd be willing to help?"

"You bet. Planning is free." Jessica held up a finger. "However, after your place is up and running, I'll be your accountant, and you'll have to pay me. And have to keep your receipts in order, and your expenses written down, and—"

Beth laughed. "Do you nag Master Z like this?"

"God, no." Jessica rolled her eyes. "The last time I tried, he was almost at the end of some mystery, and rather than *saying* that—I mean, he could have just *told* me, right?—he tied me up, gagged me, and stuck vibrating things in me and on me everywhere. And left me lying on the floor while he finished his damned book."

"Oh. My."

"Yeah." Jessica scowled. "I came so many times that I couldn't stand up when he released me. And that was so unfair. We're not in a twenty-four hour master/slave relationship, right? And then I almost broke my hand when I hit him; his muscles are harder than rocks."

Beth tried. She really did try. A snicker escaped, then a giggle, and when Jessica looked at her in disbelief, she roared with laughter. The little blonde accountant always looked so put-together and conservative. Reserved. The thought of her, naked and punching Master Z, sent Beth into an unstoppable fit of giggles.

"You are cruising for a good slap, girlfriend." Jessica huffed, then grinned. "You know, there're very few people I could tell that to and have them laugh instead of calling the cops. Or mental health." She paused and narrowed her eyes at Beth. "But next time you laugh, you die."

"Of course. I totally understand," Beth tried to smother her giggles with Coke and choked instead. "I'm very sorry. Really."

Lightning sizzled, striking somewhere in the forest, followed by a roll of thunder. The rain increased, and Beth tipped her head back to watch the downpour, reveling in the noise and the drop in temperature.

"Well, look what we have here." Master Z walked up behind Jessica and pressed a kiss to the top of her head.

Startled, Beth gasped, then relaxed, realizing that the rain had covered the sound of his footsteps.

He looked at her and frowned. "Why aren't you working?"

Dear Lord, he thought she was being lazy. Dismayed, she opened her mouth to explain and defend, then caught the laughter in his eyes. She spared a thought of pity for her friend. This Dom had a positively evil sense of humor. "Well—"

"Looks like the rain drove a rabbit onto your patio, Z. I'll catch her for you." And two big hands reached over Beth's shoulders, slid down into her low-cut top, and caught her breasts.

Fear ripped through her and choked her breath. She tried to leap away and was yanked back against the chair. A warm breath touched her ear, and a rumbling voice said, "Relax, little rabbit."

Master Nolan. She knew he'd be here. Heart hammering, she managed to ease back, not that she'd have been able to go anywhere with his arms pinning her to the chair. He bit her neck, kissed the tiny pain, and his hands ran over her breasts.

Nolan nibbled her neck, tasting salt, smelling the woman's warm fragrance lightly scented with strawberries. She wore a gold tank top under denim overall shorts. He'd never stripped a woman out of overalls; looked like fun. He cupped her perky little breasts in his hands and felt her nipples pebble to taut points. Damned shame to have to be polite and release her.

Under his hands, the thudding of her heart eased as she got over her fright. One terrified little rabbit. Anger ran through him, knotting his muscles. What he wouldn't give to meet the bastard who'd taught this woman to be afraid.

A few minutes ago, he and Z had stood on the balcony, listening to the women talk. And laugh. He'd never heard Beth really laugh, and the sound of her unrestrained giggles had hardened him like a rock.

He wanted to draw more laughter out of her and learn what made her laugh. Their meal together had pleased him more than he'd anticipated. The woman blazed like a fire, giving off heat and light…when not terrified. And he'd spent a lot of time since thinking about how her fears crippled her.

There was work to be done, and he was just the Dom to do it.

"Have a seat, Nolan, and a drink," Z said and set a root beer on the table. Reluctantly, Nolan released his captive. He glanced at the empty chair over by Jessica. Too far away from where he wanted to be.

"I'll share Beth's chair," he said and scooped the little rabbit up. She gave a pleasing squeak. He took her place and set her on his lap. Ignoring her struggles—she wasn't really trying, he noticed with pleasure—he yanked her against his chest and secured her with a hand on her hip. "You know, I don't think I want you associating with Z's sub, sugar. She's not very well-trained."

Beth straightened indignantly, ready to defend her friend, but he kept her in place with a hand on her breast. Well, he'd planned to put it between her breasts, but…oops.

Obviously annoyed by his comment, Jessica opened her mouth then closed it. She glanced at Z.

Seating himself next to Jessica, Z kissed his sub's fingers. "We're not in the club now, little one, so you may be as rude as you wish." When Jessica smiled, he added, "But Nolan does have a nasty way of settling old scores. And you *will* be in the club on Saturday."

She sat back with a disgruntled scowl. "Well, that's not very fair."

Nolan gave her a sympathetic look. "That's why I prefer being the Dom." When Beth laughed, he kissed her, enjoying the way her lips softened under his. As he drew back, he held her gaze and murmured, "Well, there may be more than one reason." She flushed, and her nipple spiked under his fingers.

"Behave, Nolan." Z took a sip of his sub's Coke. "Beth isn't here to play, remember? She works for a living. Speaking of which, what do you think of the yard?"

Nolan compared the landscaping to his memory of what it had looked like before he left for Iraq. "That's quite a difference," he said slowly. "I like it. Much less stuffy."

A tiny smile appeared and disappeared on Beth's face.

Z frowned at her. "Beth used the exact same word. *Stuffy*. But I do like the effect she's achieved, both here and in the Capture Gardens."

"What did—"

Nolan's question was interrupted by men's voices as Dan and Cullen dashed through the open gate and into the lanai. "Damn wet out there," Cullen said, shaking his shaggy head and spraying everyone with water. "Where's the beer and the cards? Are we playing down here?" He grinned at Beth and Jessica. "Are these extra treats?"

The little sub in Nolan's lap squirmed, and he tightened his grip. It was time for the next step in her education, so she might as well get used to Cullen's ways. Besides, he wanted her to see his place without being afraid. "While you're all here..."

The noise settled. "Thursday's the Fourth. I'd like to have a party at my house. My balcony has a good view of the fireworks. Just the four of us and our subs. Start around three or so and end after the fireworks."

Daniel and Cullen were free, but Z had to decline. Nolan looked down at the rabbit who had gone immobile. "Do you want me to pick you up or give you directions?"

Her big blue-green eyes lifted and he could almost read her thoughts. The automatic wariness, then the realization that others would be present. A tiny tremor ran through her before she capitulated. "Directions, please."

"Hey, Beth, Dan's a cop. Did you report your break-in to the police?" Jessica asked.

Dan turned and asked, "What break-in?" even as Nolan voiced the same question.

* * *

Damn Jessica anyway. Beth leaned against a light pole, frowning as Nolan installed a new lock on her door. Before that, he'd reframed the door with harder wood, muttering about cheap-ass materials. And he wouldn't let her pay for anything.

Being obligated to a man, any man, bothered the hell out of her. Being obligated to this man…

Still kneeling, he closed the door, turned the key, and nodded his approval when the deadbolt *snicked* open and closed. "Looks good." He rose to his feet and walked over.

She looked up, a little unnerved by the reality of him. The bright sun highlighted the laugh lines around his mouth and eyes, the scar on his cheek, his firm lips, and stern jaw line. With him, dominant was more than a term; it was who he was to the bone.

He noticed her staring and smiled, a crease appearing in his lean cheek. He held his hand out, palm up, a Dom's gesture asking for a sub's wrists, and she couldn't seem to stop from complying despite a shiver of anxiety. Would he drag her into the apartment and…

Opening her clenched fingers, he dropped the deadbolt keys onto her palm and closed her hand around them.

"Thank you," she murmured, feeling off-center. He hadn't tried anything sexual at all and acted as if they were simply friends. Only the possessive look in his eyes gave the lie to anything different. "I still think you should let me pay for the materials at least."

"No." He tilted her chin up to give her an uncompromising look. "And next time, I will hear about your problems from *you*, not Jessica."

"But…" Wasn't their relationship just a Dom/sub club thing? He didn't want more, and she didn't want more and…

"I left directions to my house on your table. Be there at three. Wear whatever you want; it won't be on long. And make sure you put on lots of suntan lotion—all over." Grasping her upper arms, he pulled her up on tiptoe and kissed her, long and deep and hard, managing to leave her feeling as possessed as if he'd tied her down. With a faint smile and a tap of his finger on her cheek, he strode away, leaving her leaning against the side of her building for strength.

Chapter Eight

On Thursday, Beth slid out of her Toyota and rested her hands on the truck hood, fighting against the urge to flee. But, hey, she was getting better at ignoring her fears. She'd made it here, hadn't she? And really, she did want to be here. With Nolan…Master Nolan…Sir…her master.

Saying his various names and titles sent odd emotions prickling through her, making her chest feel funny. There was something between them, at least on her part, something more than just a master/sub relationship. She could easily grow…fond…of him.

She shook her head and stomped on that thought. She wasn't free to become fond of anyone and never would be. Filing for a divorce would immediately paint a bull's-eye on her. Kyler had told her in graphic detail what would happen to her. She needed to remember that.

And she needed to remember how Nolan felt about a woman cheating on her husband. A little quiver of worry ran through her at the memory of his harsh face when he talked about his wife.

So absolutely no…fondness, Beth.

Right. Really, she just liked him because of what he'd done for her. Because of him, she felt more like herself than she had in years. She felt like a woman again, pretty, competent. How odd that being submissive could let her feel more competent. It was because of Sir. Although he assumed she'd naturally submit to him, he obviously believed she was still her own person. A strong person.

Since she'd been with him, her body seemed less cold. So she wasn't going to be a scaredy-cat and stop now. She trusted him...mostly... More than anyone else in forever. She'd let him take her further.

And, despite her internal pep-talk, the thought closed her throat. God, she was such a coward.

With an exasperated sigh, she moved away from the truck and finally took a good look at her surroundings. All she could do was stare. Newly built, the two-story Spanish-style house was a pale gold stucco with arched windows everywhere. A white flagstone patio extended out in a semicircle around a splashing fountain.

She hadn't nearly managed to finish gaping when Nolan walked out between the pillars of the covered portico. Her heart gave a painful thump. Dressed in blue jeans and a white, short-sleeved shirt that set off his dark skin, the Dom was as gorgeous as his house. *Look at him...* He could have any woman he wanted. What in the world was she doing here?

She felt like a terrified puppy wanting to crawl back into its kennel and could almost feel a tail curling under her belly, so she straightened and raised her chin. "Hi," she said casually.

"Hi, yourself." Not stopping at a polite distance, he walked right up to her and effortlessly lifted her high enough to kiss her, his mouth warm and demanding.

A nice blaze burned inside her body by the time he released her.

"Well." She sucked in a breath, realized she was holding his waist, and pulled her hands back. "You have a beautiful home."

"Thank you." He ran a finger down her cheek. "I'm glad you like it."

Two more trucks came up the long, winding drive. The first pulled up behind Beth's. Kari bounced out, long brown hair blowing in the slight breeze. "Nolan, Dan says you built this. It's gorgeous."

He built it? "Well"—Beth set her hands on her hips and waggled her head at him, trying to remember his exact tone—"next time, I will hear about these projects from *you*, not Kari."

God, she loved the sound of his deep laugh.

As he wrapped an arm around her and pulled her against his solid body, Beth smiled at the other two couples. Although the subs were in shorts, all the Doms were in jeans. Dan wore a tight black T-shirt. Cullen's brown and gold tropical shirt hung open, displaying his broad chest.

"Come on in." Nolan waved everyone into his house.

The inside was as lovely as the outside, with high ceilings and gleaming hardwood floors. Recessed niches in the creamy stucco walls held dark red vases with flowers. They went through the foyer, past a wide staircase with wrought iron railings, and into the great room. Colorful hand painted tiles framed the arched windows and wide doorways. More tiles accented a big stone fireplace on the far wall.

A hand-loomed rug defined the sitting area, and everyone took seats on the tan leather sofa and chairs. Nolan rested a hip on a bright tapestry draped over the arm of Beth's chair.

"Everyone, this is Deborah," Cullen said, his hand on the shoulder of a tall, muscular brunette. Beth remembered seeing her at the Shadowlands. She also was new to the club and not especially friendly. Cullen pointed to the others. "Deb, this is Daniel, Kari, Nolan, and Beth." Turning back to Nolan, he said, "Okay, Nolan, give them the bad news."

Bad news? What…

"Relax, little rabbit," Nolan murmured, tugging her hair lightly. He said to everyone, "None of you subs have participated here before, but your Doms have, although it's been over a year since I held a party."

"And it's about time you started again," Cullen said. He propped his long legs up on the coffee table.

"Subs, here are the rules: you do not need to keep your eyes lowered, but you may not speak unless asked a question. You may kneel to get permission to speak. Any Dom here may touch you or punish you with a spanking, but nothing more intense without your master's permission. No penetration without permission of your master. Your safe word is red, and that means everything stops. You may use yellow if you're having a problem, and that word may or may not be honored."

Beth glanced around the room. The Doms were leaning back, legs outstretched, totally at ease. Deborah knelt at Cullen's feet, looking bored. Kari sat beside Dan on the couch, her hands clenched in her lap, the knuckles white.

Sir had said Kari hadn't been in the scene very long. Well, that made two of them. Beth shivered. She'd only had *real* Doms for a short period, and apparently there was an awful lot she didn't know about this stuff.

Nolan tugged on Beth's hair again and pointed to the left. "There's a powder room over there where you can change. Go now."

"Big," Beth murmured as they entered. The soft pink room was the size of her studio apartment. Wrought iron scrollwork decorated the mirror over the long counters. There were even showers.

"Dan said Nolan comes from a large family and wants one of his own. I guess he designed this place for that"—Kari played with the buttons on her shirt—"and for stuff like this."

Without speaking even once, Deborah stripped casually and left the changing room.

"Why does this feel scarier than the club?" Kari asked, unbuttoning her blouse slowly.

"Because the guys are all friends and are used to playing together"—Beth bit her lip—"and we're the toys about to be played with."

Kari giggled. "What a way to put it. But, oh, so true." She folded her blouse neatly, setting it on a shelf against the dark blue wall.

Beth screwed up her courage and pulled her top off. "I hate naked," she muttered.

Kari put the rest of her clothes away before frowning at Beth. "Finish up, girl, or I'll leave you in here. And Master Nolan doesn't look like a patient Dom."

"Now that was mean," Beth grumbled. But just the thought of annoying Sir was enough to make her strip quickly. Stuffing her clothes onto a shelf, she followed the lushly curved woman toward the door. "I feel like a stick," she grumbled.

Kari turned and whispered, "And I always feel fat. Ever notice how women never like their bodies?" Their eyes met in a moment of perfect understanding, and Beth realized she was going to have another friend.

The warm feeling only lasted long enough to leave the powder room. Between the air-conditioning and the gazes of the three men, Beth felt chilled to the bone. Resisting the urge to cover her private areas, she followed Kari across the room. Yeah, this naked stuff really sucked.

Master Nolan was lounging in the chair she'd vacated. He looked her over slowly, making her feel beautiful and sexy without saying a word. His lips curved up in a way that said he liked seeing her, naked and in his home—her insides turned liquid. She halted in front of him, expecting another command. Instead, he grasped her hips and pulled her between his legs, trapping her, while his hands ran over her bare skin. Cupping her bottom, he nuzzled her stomach. "You smell good, little sub. Like lemonade and strawberries."

He nipped her hip hard enough to make her yelp, then rose to his feet. "Cullen, you two make yourselves at home.

The dungeon room's down there." Nolan pointed to a hallway running past the stairs. "Dan, our set-up is outside." Taking Beth's hand, he strolled to the back of the great room, through French doors, and onto a covered lanai. The outdoor room opened to a wide, screened patio. On the right was a dining area with built-in barbecue, table and chairs, and a hacienda-style fountain.

To the left, an Olympic-sized pool sparkled in the sun. Maroon lounge chairs lent color to the area, but Beth couldn't help but visualize how much better it would look with big pots of bright flowers. Just outside the screen by the pool, clusters of palms and palmettos really needed some ferns to transition from tall to short.

Straight ahead, an immense, heartbreakingly ugly yard of weeds led down to a small lake. Dropping Nolan's hand, she took a few steps forward. Much of the hardscape had been put in already. A beautiful stone walkway led from the house, under arching trees, and down to a small dock. Beth could hear Kari and Dan commenting on the lake but couldn't get her mind to focus on anything besides what she would plant if the place were hers.

"Don't start digging yet, sugar." Nolan tugged lightly on her hair. "I'll take you for a walk later. I'd like something on the order of what you did for Z. That wild look. Think you're up to the challenge?"

Starting from scratch in a setting this beautiful… She wanted this job so badly she was liable to start drooling like a dog. "Yes. I could do this." She smiled slowly. "I can make it absolutely gorgeous."

"Good. After supper, you can drag me around and tell me where you want to start." His confidence in her was like a heady drug, and her smile grew. First she'd start by leveling—

"Beth..." With an exasperated sound, he tangled his fingers in her hair, pulled her head back, and kissed her plans right out of her head. "Later. I need to torture you a little first."

He pulled her to a pair of heavy teak tables close to the pool. Chairs around the tables held covered trays and bowls of water. When she saw chains embedded into the table legs and top, a tickle of anxiety chased down her spine. Just how extreme did BDSM parties get?

Sir held out his hand. "Wrists, please."

With a tiny quiver, she gave him her wrists. He buckled well-padded cuffs on, then set her on the edge of the smoothly finished table. Her breathing increased as he pushed her flat, leaving her legs dangling over the end. She turned her head and saw Dan chaining Kari on the other table. The Dom was so big and muscular he made his well-endowed sub appear fragile.

Beth looked up at Nolan. That was pretty much how Master Nolan made her feel, and she liked that...most of the time.

Silently Sir chained her hands over her head and then spread her legs wide. He took a warm washcloth from the bowl of water, laying it on her pussy.

"Master?" The word seemed to come easier and easier.

He sat down beside her and curved a hand over her breast. "Have you ever shaved down there, Beth?"

Shave? She shook her head.

"Was there a reason?"

"Not really. I wasn't ready with the first Dom, and Master Chris didn't care, and then I…the last one…" Her mouth tightened. Kyler had cared only about how she presented herself in public. And how she screamed.

"You know, sugar, I get the impression your last so-called Dom was more of a sadist than a Dom. Am I right?"

"He started in BDSM, but, well… Yes. That's right."

"He got a name?" Master Nolan asked softly, running a finger down her cheek.

"I…no." She didn't want any chance of him finding her or Sir looking him up either, for that matter.

His finger stilled, his eyes dark, then a corner of his mouth drew up into a faint smile. "We'll keep working on this trust issue of yours. Meantime, you're going to have a bare pussy today, and you can tell me if you like it or not."

"Well, okay." Did he plan to shave her himself? "Sir, I can do it."

He chuckled. "But I can do it better." He walked to the foot of the table. "I'm going to strap you down tightly, little rabbit, so you can't move at a bad moment." One strap went across her stomach and another just above her hips. Then he bent her knees up and secured each thigh to the waist strap. Her pelvis tilted up.

She licked her lips, a sense of wrongness running through her. Restrained outside? Her pussy up in the air. She felt horribly vulnerable. When she looked over at the other table, she saw the same expression of dismay on Kari's face.

"Relax, sugar, I don't have neighbors. No one can see you but me and Dan." Nolan seated himself in a chair at the foot of the table. He opened a packet of disposable razors and tossed them into the bowl of water. With scissors from the tray, he clipped her pubic hair short and rubbed shaving lotion into what hair was left. A slight herbal scent drifted to her.

Even after the lotion was applied, his fingers kept stroking her outer labia until need started to rise in her, and she gave a little squirm. Lifting her head, she saw amusement in his eyes. "You don't appear to have any problems getting aroused anymore," he murmured before nibbling on her inner thigh.

Her hips tried to move against the teasing bites, but she was thoroughly restrained. The knowledge sent more heat swirling through her.

Sir said, "Now stay very still, sugar." She felt scraping on the top of her mound, each stroke followed by a splashing as he cleaned the razor in the bowl. His hands were warm and sure as he continued, finishing the top, working down her outer lips. Pulling her skin taut, he shaved further, almost to her anus, opening her as needed with firm hands.

The outside world seemed very distant. She could hear Dan murmur to Kari, soft violin music from hidden speakers, Cullen's booming laugh from inside the house. The intimate touch of Sir's fingers and the slow scraping of the razor became increasingly erotic.

"All done." Sir tossed the razor into the water and rubbed something cool onto her bare folds. "Let's see if you can tell the difference."

She gasped when his mouth touched her pussy. She could feel…everything, not just his tongue on her clit, but his cheeks against her bare lips, the warmth of his skin, and the tiny scratchiness of his chin. Every sensation was amplified. Holding her labia open with unyielding fingers, he exposed her clit and licked over it.

"Ah!" She jerked at the exquisite shock. She felt a tiny puff of air, then his hot, wet mouth. Another puff of air hit directly on her clit. Hot mouth again. Her breathing turned ragged as fire shot through her, as her clit swelled, the tiny nub of nerves straining for more.

But he moved to run his tongue over her labia. His teeth gripped an inner lip, biting gently until jolts of sensation spiraled around her core. Her hands clenched the chain binding her, and her legs strained against the straps. She could do nothing except pant and whimper as he teased her, tonguing her clit, biting her folds. He brought her right to the edge of release, then backed away.

The muscles in her legs tightened as she tried to lift into his mouth. The restraints held her securely. She couldn't move at all. She felt like a quivering, mindless doll, there for him to do whatever he wanted with her.

One finger slid into her, very slowly pushing between her swollen tissues. He pulled out and thrust two fingers in, ripping a cry from her. The intense pleasure increased, expanding to the entire *V* between her legs.

His fingers plunged in and out of her, and his tongue rubbed the sides of her clit in the same rhythm until her legs jerked uncontrollably in the restraints. Her breathing stopped, her whole body going rigid. Waiting. Needing release so badly she moaned. As everything constricted, his lips captured her clit, pulsing directly on the nub.

There was a roaring sound in her ears as she tried to arch, couldn't move, and screamed instead as she spasmed around his fingers. Each forceful contraction of her vagina shot hot waves of pleasure through her body.

She quivered as he withdrew his tongue and his fingers. "I like you bare," he murmured. "Seems like you do too." And then he stood, sheathed himself in a condom, slicked the broad head of his cock in her juices, and plunged into her straight to the hilt. She screamed and climaxed again, billowing around his huge cock in exquisite explosions.

He ran his big hands up the back of her strapped thighs, anchoring her firmly as he started to thrust. She strained against his grip, and the feeling of being overpowered shot her back into arousal and need. His black gaze moved over her face, and then he tightened his hands even further, making her moan again.

His cock plunged in and out of her in a compelling rhythm—slow, fast, slow, fast—until her body started to constrict around him again. Her newly bare lips were so sensitive that she could not only feel his cock, but the hair at its base, his slightly rough balls, the warmth of his hips. The unfamiliar stimulation drove her insane. Too many sensations for her mind and her body to process.

His fingers moved down her thighs, and suddenly she became aware of how close they were to her clit, and now each movement inside her increased her urgency. His touch moved a little closer. A finger trailed across the top of her mound as his cock slid in and out of her. His finger traced down the inside of a fold, missing her clit. She moaned in disappointment.

He slowed, drawing his cock out of her inch by inch, pushing back in, inch by goddamned inch. His finger moved toward her clit again, teasing around, but never reaching it, and she whimpered as the tenseness inside her became too full to bear.

Her hands fisted as she panted. She could do nothing to get closer, nothing to make him touch her there, and a moan broke from her. "Please, please, please..."

To her distress, he stopped moving altogether with just the crown of his cock still in her. Her head rolled back and forth as her whole body pulsed and ached.

"M-master..."

"That's right, sugar," he murmured. His cock drove home with one hard thrust. His slick finger stroked over her clit at the same time, fast and rough. The sky disappeared as she broke, screaming and screaming. Her body shuddered, convulsing around him, against him. His grip moved back to her hips, tightening painfully as he gave a guttural growl and came in violent jerks inside her, pressing so deeply she felt as if his shaft filled her entire body.

He was breathing fast and smiling as he released his grip. As she fought for breath in the humid air, he leaned down between her strapped thighs and rested his cheek on her stomach. "Listen to that little heart pound," he murmured. "I'd better give you a break before you shake apart."

He kissed her stomach, then nipped, laughing when her pussy clenched around him. Rising, he pulled out, leaving her quivering in emptiness. After disposing of the condom, he gently unstrapped her, helped her sit up, and sat beside her on the top of the table. Her head still whirled.

At the other table, Master Dan tossed the razor into the bowl. "All done here," he announced.

Beth looked at Kari and choked. He'd left enough hair on his sub's shaved mound to form the shape of a heart.

Master Nolan snorted a laugh. "You pervert," he said to Master Dan, getting a flashing grin back in answer.

Frowning, Kari lifted her head. "What? What did he do?" She got a quick slap on her thigh.

"Silence, little sub. You can admire my work later." Taking a scoop of the lotion, he started rubbing it into her folds so thoroughly that her head fell back with a groan.

"Come, little rabbit," Sir said, lifting Beth off the table and wrapping an arm around her. "Time to feed you and get you rehydrated. I think you panted away most of the fluid in your body."

She shook her head. The concern he showed for her was unsettling. How many times had she fainted after one of Kyler's so-called sessions, weak with dehydration and pain? How many times had she needed to crawl up the stairs, unable to stand? The memory invaded her mind like a maggot, and she edged closer until her body rubbed up against Sir's with every step.

Nolan felt the little sub burrow closer and ran his hand over her hip. She didn't usually snuggle. He glanced down, seeing how the tiny muscles around her lips had tensed, and her fingers had clenched. "What was that thought?"

She stiffened, and he smothered a smile. She really hated sharing her emotions.

"Beth."

"Nothing."

Anger surged through him, not surprising in the arrival, but the amount. "Beth," he snapped, and her gaze whipped up even as she flinched. He breathed out, tried to control his voice, but it still came out cold. "Lying… I have a low tolerance for lying." Another breath. "Why don't you try that answer again?"

"Yes, Sir," she whispered. "I was thinking about how…how differently you treat me than…someone else." She glanced down at the scars on her arms.

"Someone else, huh? Since you won't tell me his name, we'll call him the bastard. No, make it the cowardly bastard, since only a coward picks on a person littler than himself."

A weak laugh, but a laugh. She was still so close against him that he could feel her muscles relax. "All right." She continued in a fast flurry of words, an obvious attempt at balancing the scales. "The cowardly bastard never… It's strange to have someone notice I need water." The wonder in her voice shook him deep inside.

He stopped and wrapped both arms around her, letting her feel his warmth and his strength. "Beth, when a Dom takes control, leaving no choices for the sub, he has to see to *all* her needs, not just sexual, but emotional and physical also. If your Dom doesn't do that, then you find a new Dom."

Her lips were open, her body as relaxed as he'd ever seen it. He nuzzled the smooth curve of her neck before drawing back, lifting her chin to look into her big eyes. "And if I am not meeting those needs in any way, I expect you to tell me about it."

Her lips formed the word, "But—"

Now this was a question he'd had before. He ran his thumb along her stubborn little jaw line. "We're not in a Dom/sub relationship twenty-four hours a day, Beth, so unless we're playing or at the club, you can talk anytime you want. If we *are* playing, kneel and ask permission. I rarely refuse." He bit her earlobe and whispered, "I enjoyed seeing you kneel before me last week."

A tremor coursed through her body and made him laugh.

When they reached the kitchen, Beth stopped and stared. Dusky yellow walls with brightly painted tile accents. Dark granite counters. Appliances that would make a chef weep in joy.

He opened the refrigerator and pulled out bottled water and a platter of finger foods. Tiny sandwiches, miniature quiches, and other hors d'oeuvres were circled by slices of apples, oranges, and pineapple.

"Did you make all that yourself?" she wondered.

His smile flashed, and she realized he'd smiled more today than she'd ever seen. "Not a chance. My housekeeper does this type of fancy stuff. I asked her to come in an extra day this week and set this up." He handed her the platter.

"You are so spoiled," she told him and winced. Dammit. She'd gotten away with that question but teasing him? The laughter in his eyes said he'd been waiting for her to hang herself.

"Stay right there," he murmured. She heard the bottles drop onto the table. He stepped behind her, his hard body against her back, his hands sliding under her arms and capturing her breasts. "Don't drop the tray, sugar," he cautioned as she jerked. She tightened her hold, gritting her teeth as he played with her breasts, thumbing the nipples, pinching them lightly until they peaked. Her arms began to shake as her insides turned liquid.

He chuckled and bit the muscle just below her neck sharply. "Just remember, honey, if Cullen or Dan hear you talking without permission, they'll likely be doing this…or spanking you."

Oh, God. "Yes, Sir," she whispered.

After a final caress, he released her, leaving her breasts swollen and aching.

In the great room, he set the bottles on the coffee table along with the platter. He grabbed a blanket from a pile on one of the couches, dropped it on the floor beside a chair, and pointed to it.

Her seat, huh? And yet, as he took the chair, and she knelt on her blanket, contentment washed through her. Why was sitting at his feet so…enjoyable? Even arousing?

God knew, she never felt the urge to be submissive in everyday life. But here at this play party… Oh, yes, she liked it. As she settled, her newly bare pussy brushed against the woven blanket, and she jumped. How in the world did women who shaved wear tight jeans?

"Drink this, Beth." Nolan opened a bottle of water and handed it to her as the others joined them. Deborah settled at Cullen's feet, and Kari at Dan's. Kari kept glancing down at the heart on her mound, still obviously stunned, and her Dom's lips quirked every time she did.

"Cullen, take a look at how hard we worked," Dan said. "Stand up, Kari."

Good grief, he wasn't serious, was he? Beth tried to slide behind Nolan's legs and scowled when he rumbled, "Up, Beth."

Cullen looked them over, barking a laugh at Kari's decoration. Beth hoped her blush wasn't as obvious as Kari's, but from the amused look on Sir's face, she had a feeling they were equally red.

As they sat back down, Master Nolan told the Doms to help themselves to the food. And with each hors d'oeuvres, Sir took, he handed her one, tidbit by tidbit. After a few minutes, she noticed she was now getting only foods she liked, like the tiny quiches and the fruit, not the crab-filled shells or the yucky brie. The realization he took the trouble to notice and please her in even this small way made her feel funny. Happy. She looked up at him as she popped a grape in her mouth.

He was watching her. As the grape filled her mouth with sweetness, his eyes crinkled, and then he returned to the men's conversation.

After the food was gone, the Doms discussed the club for a bit: the changes Z planned to make, the new members, the next meeting of the Shadowlands masters at some restaurant. Nolan glanced down at Beth. "The subs also meet once a month. Did anyone tell you?"

"Jessica mentioned it, but I've never gone." She'd never felt like a normal submissive. Not until now. "Maybe I'll go next time."

"I—" Kari stopped, slid a look up at her Dom. "Permission, Master?"

"Good catch, little sub." He pulled a strand of her long hair with a smile. "Granted."

"I just went last time with Jessica," Kari said to Beth. "It was more fun than I'd thought." She gave Dan an innocent look. "We talk about how horrible our Doms are and sneaky ways to get around them. Why don't I call you that day, and we'll all go together?"

Beth nodded enthusiastically. Two friends. She had two friends now.

Chapter Nine

After a trip to the powder room, the subs followed their Doms to Master Nolan's dungeon near the front of the house. Stomach quivering with nerves, Beth lagged behind the others and stopped in the doorway. The dungeon was almost as big as the great room. It had shutters over the windows, a dark hardwood floor, dark paneling, and dim lighting. If Nolan had designed it to be intimidating, he'd done a good job. She hugged herself as chills goose-bumped her skin.

The ceiling beams were exposed with chains dangling from them. A St. Andrew's cross leaned against one wall. A bondage table, a sawhorse…more equipment in a dark corner. Various toys hung on the walls: whips, floggers, paddles, canes. The big armoire probably held others.

"I'd forgotten some of what you had here," Master Dan said, dropping his toy bag and wandering around the room followed by a wide-eyed Kari. "I'm going to have to play catch-up."

Cullen snorted. "Isn't possible. Just about the time you do, he'll build himself another piece."

Build? Venturing a few steps into the room, Beth bent to examine the closest piece, a spanking table made of solid oak. The joins were perfect, and the finish satin smooth.

Was there anything the man couldn't do?

She realized she'd spoken aloud when Sir squeezed her shoulder and answered, "I cook badly. I can't add without a calculator, can't sing a note, and anything I plant dies in a week." The gentle look in his eyes captured her gaze more effectively than any restraint.

"Got a game for us?" Cullen asked.

Master Nolan ran a finger down her face before turning to the others. "Don't I always? The game is in two parts. First, restrain your sub and warm her up in whatever manner pleases you: flogger, paddles, hands, whips."

Whips? Apprehension scraped like fingernails through her insides. She tried to edge away. Sir's fingers curled around her arm, stopping her.

"After that, we'll go out to the pool area, and our subs will serve refreshments," Nolan continued. "I'll explain that part when we get out there."

She really, really didn't like the slight smile on his face when he talked about "serving," but the worry about what he planned to do in the dungeon was more immediate.

Dan said, "I remember the game you came up with last time. You're an evil bastard sometimes."

Nolan grinned.

When Dan clipped Kari's wrists together and tugged her over to a chain, the sub looked appalled, whispering, "You wouldn't really beat me, would you? Master?"

Dan didn't stop.

Cullen strung Deborah up quickly. He visited the wall, returning with a paddle and dropping a cane on the floor nearby. Deborah took a deep breath, her face flushing and nipples peaking.

"Come, little rabbit." Sir tugged on Beth's arm, but she'd set her feet. With a laugh, he swung her over his shoulder and set her down under a dangling chain. His strength seemed frightening all of a sudden, and her mouth went dry. He hooked the chain to her wrist cuffs and winched her up until her toes barely touched.

"That is a pretty sight," he murmured, running his hands over her breasts. His palms were warm against her cold skin. He tilted her chin up. "What is your safe word, sugar?"

"Red," she whispered. "Can I use it now?"

"Do you think I'm going to hurt you unbearably?" he whispered back.

Yes. No. Maybe. Playing in the Shadowlands felt so much safer. This dungeon was too much like the room Kyler had set up. Too private, too dark. What if Sir kept her here after the others left? Everything inside of her shook. A frightening sound caught her attention, and she stared as Cullen slapped a paddle across Deborah's thighs.

Sir followed her gaze, snorted, and grabbed a blindfold from the wall. "I know you've seen that at the Shadowlands, even had it done to you, Beth. But today, you might do better not watching everything."

The blindfold wiped out the room. Now she heard even more clearly the smack of the paddle hitting flesh and the tiny grunts accompanying it, the creak of chains, a bitten-off cry from Kari and her Dom's deep laugh. She could smell lingering disinfectant, and then Sir's scent of leather and man and soap. No fancy colognes for him, he—

Something soft touched her left arm, and she jerked then relaxed at the fluffy feel. *Fur.* It moved down her arm, over her breasts, and zigzagged across her stomach to her bare mound. She held her breath as the fur stroked her, circling some areas quickly, then moving in gentle strokes across her buttocks. The touches were never where she anticipated, and slowly her skin roused.

She gasped as something cold circled her breast. Freezing water trickled between her breasts and down until her stomach muscles flinched from the icy feel. Her lips were wetted before the cold moved down her neck and across her collarbone.

Master Nolan's mouth closed around her nipple. He sucked briefly, leaving the skin tight and wet. A hand squeezed her bottom and released. She received a nip on her other breast. Each brief touch left her more sensitive. When he patted her bare pussy, need shot through her in a massive wave. He sucked her other nipple, his mouth hot and wet. When he puffed air on the wet skin, her nipple peaked almost painfully. Her breasts felt swollen.

He touched her pussy again, and this time slid his fingers through her fold. "You're wet, sugar," he whispered. With one hand gripping her bottom, he slid a finger up into her, holding in place as she jerked at the sudden intrusion. Two thrusts and then he spread the wetness over her clit, rubbing the nub slickly with a firm finger until it hardened. Until her hips tilted into his hand.

And then Sir moved away, leaving her pussy burning. Where had he gone? She listened anxiously. What was he planning now? Her heart rate climbed.

Something hit her legs, a spatter of sensation, too soft to be painful. Another and another, moving across her body slowly, each stroke like a heartbeat with only the location changing. The tiny flicks over her breasts were erotic; more teased her pussy until her clit ached with need. The blows increased, stinging now, tiny nips that hovered on the edge of pain, transforming to carnal pleasure.

Suddenly, from the right, Deborah screamed, a high shrill cry that echoed in the room.

Beth jumped at the sound, the chains clinking above her. She tried to inhale… No air came. Her lungs pumped, but she felt like someone was squeezing her chest, keeping her from getting a breath.

She heard a thump of something. "Yellow," she gasped through numb lips. "Yellow."

Sir yanked the blindfold off, and the room appeared, wavering around the edge. His fingers closed around her arms.

"Easy, sugar. Look at me," he snapped, and his unwavering gaze filled her vision. "Breathe with me. Exactly with me." A Dom's command. When he inhaled, his big chest expanded, and her own followed… In. Out. In. Out. Not enough air. Her breathing sped up. He growled, and she focused again. Breath by breath. The tightness in her chest eased, and her heart rate slowed. The room came into focus.

He cupped her face. "Better?"

She nodded. "I got scared."

He snorted. "You had a panic attack, sugar. I think I'll leave the blindfold off so you remember who your Dom is today."

"You're going to continue?" Her breathing faltered.

His hand was still on her face, keeping her gaze on his. "Were you in pain…or were you scared? Think for a minute." And he waited.

She frowned. The flogger hadn't been striking that hard and actually had been rather exciting. But the scream, the sounds around her, especially Cullen and the sound of the cane he was using, had revived old memories. Sir hadn't hurt her. "Scared, Sir. I was just scared."

His smile was slow, waking something inside her that glowed with his approval. "Honest sub." He looked around and picked up the flogger from the floor.

She realized the thump she'd heard had been him tossing it aside…even before she'd said yellow. He'd been watching her that closely. And then he'd talked to her and listened to her. He would stop if she couldn't take it. The knowledge felt good. Freeing.

Stepping back, Master Nolan shook out the flogger. When her breathing increased, he caught her gaze again. "Watch *me*, Beth, not your memories. I want your eyes on me at all times."

He waited until she managed to lift her gaze away from the instrument of pain and up to his eyes. His smile at her was like a warm hug.

He started slow and gentle again, the leather strands more of a caress than a blow with the same rhythm as her heart, brushing against her skin until she began to anticipate each blow. When he moved up her body, over her buttocks, and around to her breasts, her breathing was fast, not from fear, but excitement. Featherlight touches on her pussy, the new bareness adding to the sensation. The force increased, reaching the tiny stings where she'd panicked before, but she watched Master now.

His eyes were hot and intense, his face hard as he concentrated, not on her pain, but on her arousal. He saw her every response, and everything he did drew her higher and higher, and her response in turn carried him along. Nothing else existed except the two of them.

As if he could hear her, his smile flickered, his gaze burning over her as the strokes lightened again into teasing flicks across her mound. Her clit started to ache, and she grew so wet that it trickled down her leg.

The flogger moved up, and the strands hit her breasts with more force. She jerked in the chains as fire streaked down to her clit. Her nipples constricted into peaks just in time for the next blow. And the flogger moved away, circled around her back, lashing her bottom. Her excitement increased, her clit throbbing.

The blows became harder, hurting, and she yelped, only each strike slid from pain to pleasure so quickly that her cry turned to a moan. Two blows onto her pussy, and she rocked back at the pain, yet she was so close to a climax that her hips pushed forward to meet the next blow.

It never landed. He tossed the flogger on the ground and cupped her face between his hands. His eyes were molten darkness. "I'm regretting the game," he murmured, "because

I'd really like to bury myself deep inside you." He tangled his hand in her hair, his grip pulling her head back as he took her mouth. His tongue plunged into her over and over until her breath turned ragged.

"You cheating over there, Nolan?" Cullen's rough voice had amusement in it.

With a low groan, Sir drew back. He unfastened her from the chains and lifted her into his arms so quickly her head spun. As he carried her out to the pool, her skin was so acutely sensitive she could feel even the tiny hairs on his arms.

Beth quivered in his arms as Nolan led the others to the pool area, and he stopped long enough to nuzzle her cheek. She'd done well in accepting the flogging despite her past and that she'd been aroused by it was more than he'd expected. Her courage in admitting her fear, and moving past it touched his heart. She was a tough little woman, and she felt good—right—in his arms.

Well, hell. He'd gotten sucked right into caring for this little bundle of troubles.

Putting that worry aside, he glanced around the pool area, checking the position of the chairs and tables. Nothing missing. His gaze snagged on the weedy yard outside the patio, and he winced. If Beth didn't take on the job, he'd have to search for someone, and God knew what kind of an idiot landscaper he'd get. Probably end up with squared-off gardens in pink and white. Beth better step up to the plate, or he was going to be pissed off. He glanced down at her, smiled at the way she'd snuggled against his chest. *Be brave, little rabbit. Take a chance.*

He set her on her feet then took a towel from the stack on a table and dropped it onto the concrete beside the middle patio chair. "Sit there, sugar. I have to get something from the kitchen."

When he returned with a tray of small paper cups and drinks, the others had settled in with Doms in the chairs, subs at their feet. At the far end of the pool, Nolan filled the cups to the brim and set them in a single line across a big table. After grabbing the water, he returned to the others and handed each sub a bottle. All three had the flushed look of interrupted passion, and he smothered a grin. "Drink up."

He turned to Dan and Cullen. "Here's the rules for the second half of the game." He pointed to the baskets beside each chair. "You each have a basket of toys. We'll start with the vibrator." He reached into his basket and pulled out the garish purple and green bullet, trying not to smile at Beth's worried look. She definitely hadn't been to a play party before. "Lay back, sugar."

He could see her desire to say no, even though her nipples tightened. Slowly she lay back on the beach towel. In the sunlight, her blue-green eyes were clear as glass as she watched him warily.

"Relax. This won't hurt a bit." He grasped her ankles, spread her legs apart, and knelt between them. She was very wet. Still enlarged, her clit glistened, slightly reddened from the flogger, and just begging for attention. *Not yet.* He slid the purple bullet into her vagina. Enjoying her squirming, he made sure the curved form would hit her G-spot.

Rising, he pulled her to her feet and instructed the others. "Attach the remote to your sub on the side and out of the way." Using bondage tape, he secured the small box to Beth's waist.

Once everyone was ready, he continued. "Subs, you've been rehydrated, but your Doms are thirsty." He pointed to the other side of the pool. "There're drinks over there. Master Dan gets water, Master Cullen gets dark beer, and I get light beer. When you fetch the drinks, go in alphabetical order: Beth, Deb, Kari. Take the next cup in line and serve it to the correct master. Don't serve the wrong drink to the wrong master or that master will spank you."

Deborah had no expression, Beth still looked worried, and, he had to admit, the consternation on Kari's face was priceless. Dan was a lucky guy. "If you spill, you'll get spanked by the master whose drink you spilled. If you make it back with a full cup, the Dom will reward you with hands or mouth in whatever way he wants."

"After your reward or reprimand, return to your own master for more toys from the basket." He glanced at the Doms. "Each round, add toys and then change the remote settings to whatever speed and mode you feel would be interesting."

"Looks like fun," Dan remarked, eyes on the pretty pink cheeks of his sub. "What happens if some little sub gets off?"

"The master whose drink is delayed gets sucked off for the length of time it takes the other two to fetch another round."

Cullen let out a bark of laughter. "Not bad. Might take a while to get a drink back down here, though."

Nolan pointed to the whippy switches beside each chair. "Not too long. The last Dom to be served has a right to be annoyed and will administer one stroke of the switch…anywhere he chooses. Each round starts at the same time with the subs in a line. Subs, begin together. Cheating will be punished."

"Questions?" he waited. "No? Then set the remotes, gentlemen." Holding Beth in place, he flipped on the vibe. She jumped, the hum audible. This wasn't the quietest vibe in the world, but definitely powerful. "Go to work, subs."

The subs were an enjoyable sight as they hurried to the other end of the pool. Deborah dark and muscular. Kari soft and round with a pleasing bounce to her ass that her long hair didn't cover. Beth like a slender flame with a high, firm butt and gorgeous legs.

Nolan rubbed his chin. Seems like he hadn't had those legs wrapped around him yet. Beth's thighs wouldn't be soft like he was used to, but strong, probably grip him like a pair of pliers. Those little heels would hammer on his ass as he plunged deeper and… *Hell.* Sitting back in his chair, he wrenched his thoughts back to the subbie race.

At the table, each woman took a cup. They lined up together and set off. Each sub concentrated fiercely on her cup, trying to walk quickly and smoothly.

Deborah spilled. Nolan grinned as she realized she'd be spanked no matter what, and she might as well not be the last to arrive. She sped up, leaving the other two behind.

The other two continued on slowly, barely distracted by the vibrators inside, moving so smoothly their breasts barely wobbled. That wouldn't last long. The higher modes had random settings.

Deborah stopped in front of Nolan and handed him a half-full glass. He frowned. "You were more worried about winning than making sure I had something to drink. I'm displeased with you."

Her reaction was minimal, and his eyes narrowed. She obviously lacked the desire to please that lay at the heart of a submissive. No wonder Cullen didn't look happy. Nolan gestured to his lap, and she stretched over his knees for her spanking. He adjusted her, bottom up. She was scarcely tense at all. All right then.

Rather than restraining her shoulders with his left hand, he reached down and cupped her breast. She wasn't expecting that. He played with her breast for a minute and then grasped the nipple between two fingers, holding it just to the point of pain. "Don't move, Deborah," he warned. "Ten strokes. Count them aloud, please."

He slapped her ass, felt it jolt through her, although she didn't move. "One," she said, voice steady.

Harder with the next blow. "Two." Harder with the third. "Three"

He slid his hand between her legs, avoiding the remote wire. Not particularly wet. He pinched her nipple, felt her pussy clench, and nodded. She was more into pain than submission. So be it. His next three slaps hit full force. She yelped and yelped again when her jerk of surprise yanked at the nipple pinned between his fingers.

Much better. He turned to check on his little rabbit, and saw Beth hand her cup to Dan. Nolan studied her for a minute. Steady hands, flushed face, clear eyes. She was doing all right.

He frowned down at the sub lying across his lap. "I didn't hear you count, so I'll start over."

And he spanked her remorselessly, pausing between each swat to give her nerves a chance to recover…so the next one would hurt as much or more. Her voice rose higher with each counted blow. "Seven." He nailed her on the tender upper thigh just below her buttocks. "Eight."

And on the other thigh. "Nine." Her voice this time was just short of a sob. He waited, drawing out the suspense before the last one, and then slapped her across both buttocks on the undercurve. She let out a high shriek before gasping, "Ten."

He checked her pussy. Sopping wet. Pain slut, indeed. "All right. Return to your Dom," he said, helping her stand. She walked over to Cullen, her self-assurance markedly diminished, and her arousal markedly increased.

Kari was hurrying away from Cullen with a long red stripe on her ass from the switch. If she'd lost the race, that meant Beth should be getting rewarded. Nolan turned to his right.

Beth had her hands laced together behind her back. Dan had wrapped an arm around her and gripped her hands, securing her between his legs, keeping her breasts right in his face. Now he ran a tongue around one nipple and took it into his mouth. Beth's color was high, her breathing fast.

Nolan grinned. Now there was a submissive.

When Master Dan sucked strongly on her breast, Beth felt a tugging sensation all the way to her pussy. And then he switched to her other breast, rubbing the nipple against the roof of his mouth until the pain and pleasure mingled through her body and weakened her knees.

When he released her, she took a wobbly step back, feeling hot and confused. How could she get excited by someone besides Master Nolan? Although Master Dan was handsome—especially when he smiled—he still wasn't Sir.

Master Dan looked up at her, dark brown eyes crinkling at the edges. He ran his finger around one wet nipple sending heat through her. "Very pretty," he murmured. She looked down. Her nipples were dark red, the peaks long and pointing like pencils. "Go to your master," he said.

As Beth stepped past Kari, Dan held his hand out to his sub. "Come, sweetie, let's see what's in the basket for you."

"Oh, God," Kari said under her breath, giving Beth an anxious look.

Beth felt Nolan's gaze on her, and she hurried over. He pulled her to him, running his hands down her thighs. When he kissed her stomach, her muscles quivered. Master Dan's touch had been as firm and controlling as Sir's, but Sir's felt…right. How could there be that much difference?

Master Nolan opened a package from the basket and held up two tweezer-like things with dangling stones. Jewelry? Nipple clamps, she realized. "Wasn't it nice of Master Dan to get you ready for these?" Sir said. "Lean forward."

He attached the rubberized ends of one clamp to a peaked nipple and moved the tiny ring upward to tighten the clamp until she hissed in pain. He lowered the ring slightly and then did the other breast in the same way. "Very pretty, sugar, don't you think?" With a finger, he made the dangling jewels swing, shooting little darts through her.

"Yes, Sir," she whispered.

Kari had also received a nipple clamps. On the left, Deborah was bent over in front of Cullen. When the sub straightened, her mouth was twisted. Beth stared at the slight dimpling around the crack of the woman's buttocks. Oh, Lord, had she gotten a butt plug? Poor Deborah.

And Deborah's bottom was horribly red. Nolan must have spanked her really hard. *Really hard.* Maybe he wasn't as…maybe he'd do… She bit her lip as her feeling of rightness eroded right out from under her.

His eyes narrowed. Then he glanced at Deborah. "Ah, little rabbit." He pulled Beth down on his lap.

She sat for a moment, confused. Even knowing he'd hurt Deborah, she still wanted to just snuggle against his chest. How wrong was that? She pushed against his chest, and his grip tightened.

"Beth, listen to me. People are different in how much pain they like and tolerate. Can you agree with that?"

"Um. Yes." That was common knowledge.

"Good. Now for you, if you're already excited, a little pain enhances your arousal."

A little unnerved by him seeing that so clearly, she looked down.

He raised her chin. "Unlike you, for Deborah, the pain *is* the arousal. A lot of pain." His intent eyes kept her from looking away. "Sugar, can you trust me to know the difference between you?"

"Yes, Sir," she whispered, and relaxed as she realized she hadn't been wrong about him. And that she could trust him. She did.

"Good." After setting her on her feet, he pressed something on the remote control at her waist. The vibrations inside her became stronger, then increased in speed, slowed…sped up again. The feeling was no longer something she could ignore.

"Next round," Nolan called, slapping her butt, making her jump.

She hurried back to the other side of the pool, the jewelry swinging from her breasts and dragging at her nipples. The feeling was a little painful, a lot exciting.

The other two waited for her to pick up the first cup before taking theirs in order. She had dark brown liquid with the malty scent of beer so it went to Cullen. The three lined up and started off, Deborah much slower this time, Kari faster. Beth ignored them and concentrated on moving steadily until she realized she was behind. Oh, God. She hurried faster, and the beer sloshed over the top, wetting her fingers. Damn, damn, damn.

Okay. Moving much quicker—what was there to lose after all—she went past the other two and heard an exclamation from Kari as she also spilled. And they both left Deborah behind.

Beth walked up to Cullen, skirting his long legs. His green eyes crinkled at her. "Little Beth, what did you bring me?"

She handed him the paper cup, and he sucked it down. A tiny hope rose in her. Maybe he hadn't noticed she'd spilled. Then he turned her hand over, raised his eyebrows at her beer-dampened fingers, and patted his lap. "Bottoms up, love."

She couldn't do this, let him hurt her. Heart pounding, she took a step back and shook her head. He didn't move, just watched her, the stern expression in his eyes so much like Sir's that her mouth went dry. He held his hand out, and she set her fingers in his before she could stop herself.

He pulled her forward gently, positioned her beside his legs, and pulled her down over his knees. She went rigid, her breathing fast and shallow.

"Relax, sweetie. It's only my hand, nothing else," he said, his hand pressing her shoulders down until her palms pressed flat on the concrete. The nipple clamps swung freely, bobbing against her face. To her surprise, he didn't start spanking her. Instead he played with her bottom, running his finger along the crack and across the crease of her thighs until she relaxed.

"Good girl. I want to hear you count and thank me for each stroke."

She remembered her first master had asked that. The memory had been buried under the horrible intervening years. A hand hit her butt, lightly, the mildest slap. "One. Um, thank you. Sir," she said breathlessly.

Another. "Two. Thank you, sir." Another and then he was hitting her hard enough to sting, alternating buttocks. Her bottom began to burn. Between each smack, she became aware of the vibrator humming inside her, and the pain made the vibrations stronger… She was very wet. Her clit started to throb, and she squirmed a little.

He stopped suddenly. She gasped when his thick fingers slid between her legs, through the folds, and pressed against her clit. The burn in her bottom and his finger on her clit joined somehow, and her hips moved involuntarily, wanting more of…something.

He chuckled. "I think you've had enough, little Beth." As easily as Sir, he set her on her feet, pinning her between his knees until her mind cleared, and her eyes could focus. She looked up to see Master Nolan's gaze on her. He'd been keeping an eye on her, and somehow she wasn't embarrassed. She just felt safe.

His eyes crinkled at her, and then he returned to the sub, Kari, lying across his lap. He swatted her two times, not very hard.

Beth turned back to Master Cullen. He smiled at her, his eyes very green in the sunlight. "Okay, love, my hand is tired. Head on back to your master."

This time Deborah had a stripe on her ass, so she must have lost the race. As Beth reached Master Nolan, Kari was climbing off his lap, rubbing her butt, tears teetering in her eyes. Her face was flushed and nipples erect. Sir held her for a moment and checked her steadiness. "Back to Master Dan with you."

As Kari hurried away, he held his hand out to Beth and pulled her to him. Turning her, he checked her bottom, running his fingers gently over the burning skin. His voice sounded amused as he said, "Well, Master Cullen must like you; he went very light."

He picked up another toy from the basket and opened it. More jewels dangling from a long narrow Y-shaped object which had a long, thin chain. Another breast clamp? She already had two…

"Lay on your back," he said.

"What? Wait—"

He gave her a look that sent her onto her back. He worked the bend in the clamp to loosen it before kneeling between her legs. When his fingers grasped her clit, she jumped. *No!* "No, Sir. Please. I—"

His raised eyebrows and silence stopped her tongue. As if she hadn't spoken, he continued and slid the bend over the top of her clit, the long sides pushing her labia together. She smothered a groan. The pressure was painful…thrilling…painful. He watched her for a moment and then nodded. "Good. Up you go."

She started to sit up and squeaked when pressure hit her squished clit. She rolled over instead and pushed to her feet. Master's eyes gleamed with laughter although he didn't smile.

He pulled her closer. When he picked up the tiny chain, she saw it ended in a *Y* shape. He secured each end to one of her nipple clamps, then tightened the tension until it was pulling up slightly on her clit and down on her breasts. Until each movement sent a shock through her.

He sat back in his chair, looked her over, and nodded. "Very nice. Breathe, sugar."

She inhaled, and the chain tightened, making her jump. Her scowl increased the laughter in his eyes. He turned her sideways and changed the settings on the remote. This time the vibrations came in long surges, reaching an intense peak that sent her close…too close to coming. Pulled chain or not, she couldn't keep from panting.

"Don't come, sugar," he cautioned her, a crease appearing in his cheek. *Damn him.*

"No, Sir," she said, trying not to moan as her insides vibrated and heat swelled through her. The thing on her clit made it worse, as if someone's fingers were pulling on her. Her knees felt like melted rubber as she walked back to the drink table.

Deborah had acquired nipple clamps. From the way Kari walked, she had a butt plug. Stepping up to the table, Beth picked up the next drink in the line. Brown—Cullen again. Something nearby hummed loudly, and Kari moaned, her face reddening.

When the other two picked up their drinks, Beth said, "Let's go."

Halfway to the men, her vibrator surged inside her, and she stopped dead, her insides coiling tighter and tighter. No, she couldn't. The others were almost to the Doms. Beth tried to move and stumbled. Her breasts bounced, pulling her clit and… *Oh, God!* The orgasm rushed over her as unstoppable as a breaking wave. Her surroundings blurred, disappearing entirely as her body shook…and shook.

After what seemed forever, she opened her eyes. She didn't remember closing them. She was still on her feet. All three Doms were watching, she realized, and felt herself turning red. Redder. If that was even possible. When she managed to start walking again, each little movement sent aftershocks through her.

When she finally got to Cullen and held out his drink, his laugh boomed across the patio. She looked down. She'd crushed the little cup completely. Cullen tossed the cup on the ground, and then shut off her vibrator. "Time to give you a rest from this."

"Thank you, Sir," she whispered, glancing at Master Nolan.

He had Kari in front of him and was lifting one of her feet to rest on the chair beside him. As if he felt Beth's gaze, he met her eyes and shook his head. "Little rabbit. You came without permission. You spilled Master Cullen's drink. And you were last. You're in for it, sugar."

He glanced at Cullen. "Toss Dan a package from the basket. He can put it on Deborah and adjust her settings. You'll be busy with Beth, I think."

Beth's legs started to tremble, and she barely managed to suppress a whimper.

Master Cullen leaned forward and took her hands, engulfing them entirely between his. He massaged her cold fingers. "Do I really look like such an ogre?" he asked, his eyes gentle.

She shook her head, realizing he wouldn't hurt her, yet still feeling the firmness in his grip, seeing the determination in his face. Nice or not, he was still a Dom.

"You may choose what to do first." His green eyes crinkled. "Choose now."

Pain, pain, or no pain. That was an easy choice. She dropped to her knees and started unfastening his jeans.

Chapter Ten

Cullen felt the little sub's hot mouth close over the head of his cock. He leaned back in the chair, pinning her between his legs, enjoying the feel of her trim little body. Her head moved as she slid up and down his cock, her delicate hands holding him firmly at the base and moving in counterpoint to her mouth. Damn, she was really good at this.

She knew it too, he realized, watching her relax, muscle by muscle, as she worked him. He glanced and saw the other girls had been sent to fetch more drinks. Deborah still hadn't come. Hell, she didn't even look very excited. He frowned. She'd been a mistake, and he'd read her completely wrong, not something he did often.

New to the club, she'd seemed pretty much to his taste. He preferred big women, ones he didn't have to worry about squashing, and she'd played the part of a submissive quite well. If he'd taken her at the club, or even spent a little time with her, he'd have seen it was an act.

Anxiety evidently conquered, Beth started sucking hard, yanking his attention back to her actions. Damn nice. Cullen tangled his hand in her hair and held her head firmly enough that she felt controlled. The pink of arousal rose into her cheeks. Unlike Deborah, Beth was submissive to the bone.

Deborah, however, liked pain for pain's sake. He'd give her what she needed today, but that would be the end of it. He knew a couple sadists at the Shadowlands, and he'd make sure they met her.

Just as he was getting into his blowjob, Deborah arrived, beer in her hand, looking very self-satisfied. First to arrive, no spills. All right then, he'd reward her…

He looked down at Nolan's pretty redhead. She'd gotten him damned close to the edge and was really challenging his control. Nolan was a lucky bastard. Beth might be full of anxieties and hang-ups, but she was a sweetheart. He tugged on her hair, "You're done now, love."

She drew back, frowned at his cock. "You didn't—"

"Time's up." He picked up the switch. "Bend over, and I'll give you your punishment for being last. Then Master Nolan can deal with you spilling my drink."

Worry flashed in her eyes, and he almost grinned. He'd been very easy on her with the spanking, not wanting to unleash buried fears. But Nolan would know exactly how far he could press his sub, and his hand might not be nearly as light. "Bend and hold your ankles."

When she complied, he gave her a stinging flick of the switch on her upper thigh, placed low enough that Nolan could swat it if he wanted, but out of the way if he didn't.

She didn't let out a sound. "Good girl. Give me a kiss as a thank you, and then go to your master."

As he took her lips, her mouth was soft, swollen from sucking on him, and tentative. He took the kiss deeper, far enough to see that she enjoyed his touch. If he ever found himself a more permanent sub, maybe he'd talk Nolan into playing some games.

He drew back, smiled at her confused look, and pushed her toward Nolan. Then he looked up at Deborah. "You did well and came in first with no spills."

Her smile was almost smug.

His was too. "So let me reward you." He swung the switch back and forth and listened to it whistle in the air. Her eyes fixed on it, her expression avid as a dog sighting a meaty bone. "Bend over, grab your cheeks, and hold them open."

Kari had already left when Beth stopped in front of Master Nolan. When he raised his eyebrows, she didn't even consider lying. "Master Cullen said for you to s-spank me."

His mouth curved in a faint, hard smile, one that made her heart give a throb and her pussy dampen. Just from his smile. "I can think of nothing I'd enjoy more," he said softly and patted his knees.

Oh, God, her butt was still tender from Cullen's spanking even though he hadn't hit her that badly. But her skin was sensitive...one of the reasons Kyler liked to—

"What was that thought?" Sir asked, stopping her as she bent.

"Noth—"

He gave her that look of displeasure.

"Ky—uh, that bastard liked my skin because it marked up nicely."

A glint of anger, his lips flattened, and then Sir shook his head at her. "I'm not into permanent marks, sugar, but I think you'll find pink is a nice…hot…color," he said easily.

There was something in his face, like he meant more than just color. He moved his legs apart, drawing her down over just his left leg. Ruthlessly, he shifted her until her butt pointed into the air. He put his right leg over the top of one of her ankles. Sir pushed her thighs apart, opening her. Her clit chain rubbed against his leg, the clamp sending painful, fiery jolts through her every time she moved. At least the damned vibe was off.

And then it suddenly came to life, and the powerful, surging vibrations almost sent her over. She stiffened, forcing the climax back. His fingers ran through her wet folds, adding to the sensation building inside her.

"Sir!"

"Be silent, sub. You don't have permission to speak," he said, his tone absentminded. His fingers slid over the top of her clit, over the nub just below the clamp, and she moaned as the need in her grew, as her body tightened. When he moved his hand away, leaving her on the edge, she whimpered.

And then he spanked her with stinging blows, leaving just enough time for the sting to dissipate before the next. One cheek, the other, back and forth. As each slap made her move and jostle the clamp, fire shot through her clit and her pussy, and suddenly she was screaming, writhing on his knee as she came, over and over and over.

When the vibrator switched off, she just lay over his knee, limp and exhausted. Panting. Her body twitched. Her bottom stung. He rubbed a finger against the mark where Cullen had switched her, and her pussy spasmed again. She moaned.

"Now, don't you think pink can be hot?" he murmured, amusement in his voice.

"That sounded rather nice." Dan's voice. "You know, I'm very thirsty. Kari, bring me two of my cups of water and run back this time."

"Sir. If I run—"

"Go now."

A definite whine came from Dan's sub.

Beth realized her bottom was up in the air. She moved and received a slap on her burning bottom that made her hiss.

"Doms. At this point, you may finish the game in any way you want," Nolan said. "I'll start the barbeque in a while, and we'll eat."

"No hurry," Dan said. "I think Kari just spilled one of my drinks."

Cullen didn't answer, but Beth could hear the sound of a switch hitting flesh and gasps from Deborah.

Sir lifted Beth up, setting her on her feet. "Spread your legs, sugar." She looked at him suspiciously, but widened her stance. He removed the remote from her waist and slipped the vibrator out of her; the feel of his hands made her pussy clench.

Picking up her towel, he took her hand and led her to the shallow end of the pool. He dropped the towel on the edge. "Sit right there, Beth." After stripping off his jeans, he jumped into the pool with a splash. The surface of the water rippled against his balls, just below a massive erection. She couldn't seem to take her eyes from his cock. It looked different in the daylight. Huge, with the skin stretched and the veins bulging. He applied a condom, and somehow it looked even bigger.

He was going to take her now, she knew, and yet her fear had disappeared. Only anticipation remained. She smiled at him.

"Well"—cupping her face between his hands, he kissed her lightly—"that is just the look I've been wanting to see." He kissed her again, then said, "Lie back now."

When she did, he gripped her hips and pulled her to the edge of the pool so her legs dangled down on each side of him, her feet splashing in the cool water. Her buttocks were right on the edge.

"Now's the hard part. Prepare yourself," he murmured. She looked at him in confusion until his hand grasped her left breast. He removed the nipple clamp.

The rush of blood to the area was agonizing, much worse than when it had gone on. She hissed through her teeth, pressing her hands over the pain.

He took her wrists, raised them over her head, and locked the cuffs together. "Leave them there." His eyes were dark, his face flushed with heat and hunger. Holding her wrists with one hand, he took her breast in his mouth, swirling his tongue around the aching nipple, making it throb. Making her throb. She whimpered.

He removed the other clamp, held her wrists until the fiery pain subsided, and then licked over that nipple. The stroking of his tongue against the tender flesh hurt yet was incredibly exciting. Her pussy began to burn. How could he possibly arouse her again?

Her breasts were jutting points when he finished, and her body tense. "Are you ready?" he asked, and she didn't know what he meant until she felt his hands touch her clit and realized he was going to—

"No!"

He chuckled. "Oh, yes." He opened the clit clamp and slid it off, then held her hips down as she moaned. The blood surged back into her clit, filling it, engorging it until the swelling was unbearable. Her leg muscles quivered as she tried to move. And then his mouth was there, his tongue circling the unbearably sensitive nub, and she screamed as his tongue flickered over it, the fever he created increasing the burning pain.

He stood upright, looked at her with those unreadable eyes, and smiled slowly.

Now wasn't she a sight to warm the heart of a Dom? Nolan thought. Eyes glazed, face flushed. Half panting, half moaning. Her nipples were erect and red as the crimson roses in Z's gardens. He caught the faint fragrance of strawberries and lemon when he bent to kiss her stomach. After running his hands down her hips, he opened her labia to expose her clit further. Unhooded, glistening, the deep color of the nub matched her nipples, and the scent of her passion surrounded him, the taste lingering on his lips. "Yes, I think you're ready. Don't you?"

He doubted she even heard him, all her attention was on her throbbing clit and not on him at all. He swirled the head of his cock in her ample juices, pressed her dangling legs more open, and drove his cock into her with one fierce thrust.

Her cry of shock echoed around the pool, and he felt her pussy billow around him. Eyes wide-open now, she stared up at him. Her hands came down as if to push him away, and he snapped, "Keep your arms over your head, sub."

Her pussy clenched at his tone, his words. Submissive. And her reaction made him harden more if that were possible. Holding her gaze with his, he started to move, watching her pupils dilate as her overly stimulated pussy began the climb up to full arousal. Over her head, her tiny hands fisted.

God, she felt good. His cock, denied for so long, seemed to feel each stroke into her hot cunt, every little twitch and clench amplified along his nerves. Deeper, he wanted deeper, wanted to bury himself so far into her he'd never see daylight again. Moving her leg, he set his foot onto the lower gutter running around the inside of the pool. Leaning forward, he gripped her hips and slammed into her, the downward tilt of her hips matching his upward thrusts perfectly. She gave soft grunts with each stroke, and he could feel her flexing around him, feel the quivering of her legs as she approached the edge.

Too soon. He'd waited so long that she'd pull him over with her if she came, and he wanted a long ride. He eased off, rocking against one side, then the other. She keened a protest, her head rolling back and forth, and he grinned. Responsive, hot, little sub.

Releasing her hips, he slowed further, taking the time to run his fingers over her bare pussy lips, enjoying the new silken feel and the way her breath hitched as her vagina clamped down on him. He teased her, sliding his wet fingers up toward her engorged clit, not touching, back down, over and over until she groaned. Until her whole body shook and she sobbed incoherent pleas.

Her pussy tightened even further, a vise around his cock, and he couldn't stand it any longer. He pulled almost all the way out, then slammed into her, burying himself, yanking back out, hammering her. With one hand, he dug his fingers into her ass, yanking her against him with each thrust. And when he was close, so close that every thrust screamed with pleasure, he slid his fingers over her unhooded clit, circled over and on top, and she let out a series of high shrieks, her pussy clamping down on him so hard, he came in a rush, jerking as she milked him dry.

Eventually he pulled out. She sighed a protest but didn't move. Poor little rabbit. He disposed of the condom and dried off enough to yank his jeans back on. Looked like Dan and Kari were busy enough…she was sitting on him, facing away, and from her gasps, well impaled. Cullen and Deborah had disappeared, probably back into the dungeon for more pain therapy.

His guests were doing all right on their own. Nolan scooped Beth into his arms and took a chair on the far side of the pool. She nestled down in his lap. Light, fragile, with a spine of iron.

Her hand rubbed over his chest, sliding under his open shirt to stroke his bare skin. It pleased him immensely that she was comfortable enough to touch him on her own.

Her pale skin was beautiful with little freckles scattered down her shoulders and arms. And so very soft. He ran his hand over her hip, enjoying the sight of his dark bronze against the white. When he nuzzled the top of her head, her soft hair ruffled his cheek. "I love watching you get off, sugar. You're over-the-top gorgeous."

She stirred a little, but didn't say anything. It was amazing how some subs chattered away during aftercare, almost as if they'd downed a bottle of wine. And with others, getting their reactions required some well-applied plastique. Good thing he'd been a demolitions expert. "I hadn't used a flogger since I got back. I'd forgotten how much fun it was."

Silence. A slight tenseness in the hand curled on his chest.

"I'm pleased you were brave enough to continue. I didn't want to stop."

"But you would have," she said finally. "If I'd wanted down, you would have released me." Her voice held enough certainty that he knew they had the first foundation block of trust.

"Yes, Beth. If you hadn't been able to overcome your fear, I'd have stopped right then." He kissed the top of her head, watched her hand flatten on his chest. Her fingers slid over his nipple and around his side. His cock stirred. If she kept touching him, he'd end up taking her again. "So, how did you like the flogger?"

"I… You know, we don't have to talk about everything. You already know how I felt. You know everything, dammit."

He smiled at the tiny flash of temper. Yeah, she'd be a fun one after those fears were gone. "We talk for two reasons. I may know how you felt, but you need to know too. Bodies and emotions don't always communicate. And secondly, I might think I'm God, but I'm not. I make mistakes just like everyone else. Now answer me. How did you like the flogger? I know you were scared, but beyond that?"

"I liked it," she admitted, pleasing him again. "I didn't think I would, but you didn't hit me that hard at first, and then when you did, it hurt, but it didn't really, or something. Every time it hit, things… I got…hotter. The spanking did that too."

He ran a finger over her flushed cheek. "Good girl. I like hearing how you felt." And she liked to hear of his pleasure, he saw. The tiny line between her eyebrows disappeared, and her hand made longer strokes on his chest. "How about when Dan sucked on your breasts?"

Her whole body stiffened, just slightly, but with her draped over him, he couldn't miss something like that. Her small fingers stopped moving, in fact, he could feel the tiny pinpricks of her nails against his skin. He'd had a feeling about this, but had been too busy to watch her closely enough.

"I liked it in a way, but I'm glad it didn't…he didn't…that he didn't touch me lower. With his mouth." He could see her brows draw together in confusion. "I don't know why."

"You usually take a different Dom at the club every week, so you're used to strangers," he prompted.

"I know. But"—her arm slid around his side, and she pulled him a little closer—"it just didn't feel right or something. I'm with…"

With me. "You feel like you're mine, and no one else should touch maybe?"

Her head went down, but her arm didn't loosen. "Pretty dumb, huh."

He tilted her head back up, looked into her confused eyes. "Feelings are feelings. They don't have dumb or smart labels, sugar. Doms have different lines that they're not comfortable letting another Dom cross. For me, I would be uncomfortable seeing another Dom's cock inside you." He rubbed his thumb on her soft cheek. "I didn't like watching you being taken by that asshole at the club."

"Oh." She tried to look away; he didn't let her.

"So when we're together, oral sex with someone else would be a no for you. How about being touched? Imagine Cullen's hands on your breasts…" He released her chin, set his hand on her breast, and thumbed the nipple.

No stiffening, in fact her breathing increased just a tad. "I…maybe…"

"Okay. We have a couple hard limits here. We'll work our way back and discuss your reactions afterward." Oddly enough, his reaction right now was satisfaction. Damned if he wasn't a little pleased that she didn't want another man's mouth on her pussy. He wrapped his other arm around her, snuggled her closer to him, and she went boneless, letting him mold her against his body. "You please me very much, Beth."

He held her as contentment hummed through him.

Kari's contentment disappeared in a rush when Cullen and Deborah returned. The big sub walked stiffly across the patio. Red welts covered her back and legs, with some even on her breasts. Beth gasped and tried to push herself off Nolan's lap. Dammit, no woman should be treated like that. She was going to—

Nolan yanked her back against him. "Easy, Beth. Look at her face, not the marks on her body."

Held so tightly she couldn't move, Beth didn't have much choice. She forced her gaze up to Deborah's face and saw what he meant. The sub might be hurting, but her face looked like a woman who'd just gotten off. Thoroughly. And from the adoring way she gazed at Cullen, she was happy with what he'd done.

"But… I don't understand," Beth said. "He hurt her."

"She likes pain."

No one likes pain. "That's just wrong."

"People have a right to their kink, sugar, as long as one person isn't forcing another," Nolan murmured in her ear. "Lots of people would say what we did earlier was wrong too."

Well, that was true. She rolled her eyes. "I'm a hypocrite, aren't I?"

"And a brave little rabbit to try to take Cullen on." He chuckled and bit her earlobe. "But take a good look at Cullen now. Deborah is well satisfied. Does Cullen look pleased with his work?"

Oh, he didn't at all. His face was strained, the lines there drawn deeper. He watched Deborah, obviously worried about her pain. More worried than the sub was. "Oh."

"Yeah. He doesn't like handing out that much pain, no more than I do. He hasn't had a good day, so be nice to him, sugar."

As Beth's anger disappeared, she leaned back against Sir, enjoying the feel of his strong arms around her. She watched Cullen, and her heart suffered at his silence. Cullen was never quiet. When Deborah disappeared into the house, Beth twisted to look at Sir. "He looks like he needs a hug."

"He does, doesn't he?" His arms opened, releasing her.

She crossed the patio to where Cullen stood, staring out at the lake. He seemed so lonely that her chest squeezed. She looked up at him, as always a little startled at his size, even taller than Master Nolan.

He finally realized she was there and turned to face her. His eyes narrowed, and he tilted her chin up. "Little Beth, what's the matter? Is Nolan being mean to you?"

Typical Dom, able to read her like a book. "Nothing's wrong. I just came over to give you a hug." She put her arms around him and gave him the best hug she could. A second later, his arms wrapped around her, and he squeezed back.

She didn't move, just rested her cheek on his wide chest, and ever so slowly, his muscles relaxed. Eventually, he took a deep breath and released her. "Thank you, love. I needed that more than I can say." Cupping her face in his huge hands, he kissed the top of her head. "Now go back to Nolan before he digs out his rifle."

She gave him a smile, pleased to see some of the strain gone from his face. She ran back to where her Master waited for her. He'd get a hug too.

Chapter Eleven

Master Nolan did up a good barbeque, Beth thought, looking down at the grilled steak, baked potato, sweet corn, and salad that he had piled on her plate. *And he said he cooked badly*. Then again, most guys probably considered grilling as the end to a good hunt, not as cooking.

Once served, the men had settled into chairs near the barbecue, talking comfortably about sports. Beth sighed. Men and their sports.

Kari and Deborah were already seated at their Dom's feet and looking bored. Beth caught Kari's gaze and jerked her head toward the other table on the patio.

Kari brightened then frowned, her eyes sliding up at Dan. Permission would have to be obtained, obviously. *Hmm.*

Beth set her plate on the ground and walked over to Sir. Stopping in midsentence, he raised his eyebrows.

Keeping her face solemn, she knelt on the concrete. "Please, My Liege. Could the subs eat together and indulge in girl-talk? Please, Sire?"

Sir choked on a laugh.

"Damn, Nolan, how'd you accomplish that?" Dan asked. "I can barely get Kari to say master."

Sir crooked a finger at Beth. When she rose, he pulled her between his knees, his hands massaging her tender bottom as he studied her face. "You're a dangerous little sub, aren't you?" he murmured for her ears only. He glanced at Kari. "Sweet and stubborn, the both of you. I can see why you get along.

"All right with you, guys?" Nolan asked. Dan grinned down at Kari and nodded. When Cullen looked at Deborah, she shook her head no.

"Just the two of you then," Nolan said.

"Really?" Beth asked. "You don't mind?"

Sir smiled, and his warm gaze made her feel…cherished. "How could I say no when you asked so nicely? Go ahead, sugar."

Kari and Beth took their food over to the table. As they talked, Beth discovered Kari and Dan hadn't been together very long, and he'd just moved into her house last week. Hearing how a normal couple—normal BDSM couple not in a full master-slave relationship—lived was an eye-opener. Dan helped out in the kitchen and with the housework.

Kari giggled, telling how after changing the bed linens, Dan had slipped into the master role, stripping Kari naked so he could enjoy her on the clean sheets.

At the thought of Nolan doing that, Beth had barely managed to hide her envy.

After everyone was finished eating, Nolan handed out more drinks and led the way to the second-floor balcony. Back to protocol, the men took chairs, and their subs had blankets at their feet.

The men talked idly, breaking into laughter every now and then. Cullen's mood had bounced back to normal, and his bellow of laughter probably scared every bird in the neighborhood. But the voice Beth listened for was Sir's. The sound of his rough voice was…comforting, like there was safety wherever he was. Well, some safety…he certainly had an awful lot of sneaky tricks up his sleeve. She shifted uncomfortably on her blanket. Her bare pussy was sensitive, her abused clit even more so. She glanced up at him with a wry smile, and he caught her gaze. His dark eyes softened as he set his scarred hand on her head and stroked her hair.

Something tugged inside her, a kind of happy recognition, like when she'd been five and wandered too far and walked and walked, and then turned a corner and saw home.

She was happy, she realized. In fact, she'd felt happier today than in…in years. Oh, she got contentment and satisfaction from her work, and pleasure in her growing friendship with Jessica, but being with Nolan was different.

She could really care about him.

And that was just way too risky, but right now, she couldn't find it in herself to worry. Not with his fingers sliding through her hair, and the scent of him on her skin.

Across the lake, small fireworks flashed in the darkness, a prelude to the big city show. "Not much longer," Nolan said. "Come here, sugar. Let's see how good you are at setting off a different kind of fireworks." He set her on her knees, facing him. With a finger under her chin, he smiled into her eyes and traced a finger over her lips. "I want that soft mouth of yours around my cock."

She blinked, a little confounded by the bluntness of his request…no, his *command.* Just like that? With everyone else watching? She tried to turn and look at the others, but his hands prevented it. "Look only at me, sugar. You may begin now."

Definitely an order, though he hadn't raised his voice. He never did, she realized. Never had to. Not with that powerful, gravelly voice. Even as she leaned forward to unbutton his jeans, shivers were running through her, and she'd become wet.

She released the last button, and his cock sprang out, thick and long. Her hands stroked over him, the satiny soft skin already tight over the rigid shaft beneath. This time it was her turn to torture him. To please him…

She licked over the round tip, tasted the drop of precum, and swirled her tongue around him. Her first Dom might not have taught her everything about BDSM, but he'd taught her plenty about how to please a man with her mouth. She moved down his cock, taking her time, tracing the big veins with her tongue, setting her teeth ever so lightly at the underside at the base, hearing his slight inhalation. She laved his heavy balls, pulling each one into her mouth to suck gently, tonguing between them before working her way back up his cock. And then, she slid him, hard and fast into her mouth, feeling his jerk of pleasure.

She worked him for a minute using only her lips and tongue until his thigh muscles tensed. Suction then suck and slide. She added her hands at the base, taking a narrow grip, sliding her hands up and down in counterpoint to her mouth. She set up a forceful, driving rhythm and heard him groan, felt him swell under her hands.

Then his hands were on her shoulders, easing her back. "Stop, you little minx. I want to finish inside you." As she lifted her head, he handed her an opened condom, and she sheathed him, enjoying the small task. She took her time, making sure it was on thoroughly, and feeling for any wrinkles until he groaned again and yanked her right off the ground.

He made her straddle his knees and then pulled her forward. His kiss was hard and demanding, and his hand in her hair kept her from moving. Knowing she was his right now, and he could take his pleasure in any way he wanted, made her hot inside.

His free hand roamed down her body as he kissed her. He played with her breasts, pinching the nipples to spikes. Spreading his legs apart slightly made room for his hand to slide under her. With no warning, he pushed a finger right into her. She gasped at the shock of his entrance, but his hand gripped her hair as he kept her in place. Her tissues were swollen from the play earlier and from her increasing arousal now.

Even as he deepened his kiss, his finger moved in and out of her vagina, and his thumb slid over her clit. His strokes were rough, as demanding as his mouth, and she tightened immediately, clenching around him.

He drew back, chuckling, then picked her up and set her on her feet. "Hands on the rail, sugar, and stay still." She leaned over and grabbed the hip-high, wrought iron railing. He yanked her hips back toward him, stretching her out, only her hands holding her up. He gently kicked her feet farther apart, opening her. Her breath quickened, and she checked her grip on the railing, expecting him to thrust into her.

Instead, he leaned over, resting his chest against her back. His arm flexed around her hip as he moved his right hand down to cup her mound. His fingers slid through her folds, spreading her wetness over her exquisitely sensitive clit, sending shudders through her body. She was startled when his left hand massaged her buttock. His fingers trailed down her crack and plunged into her vagina. Now both of his hands worked her, front and back.

Her knees started to tremble as increasing need burned through her. One of his fingers withdrew to circle her opening as his other finger circled her clit, never pressing hard enough. The throbbing increased until she couldn't think, just feel.

Her hips moved, thrusting forward uncontrollably.

"I said, 'Don't move.'" With a *tsking* sound, he stepped away from her, and a whimper broke from her lips. The stinging slap against her tender bottom made her jump and yelp.

Chuckling, he secured her hips with firm hands, holding her immobile. She felt his cock press against her, the head sliding just a little way in. And then he drove into her so hard and fast he raised her onto her tiptoes.

"Uhhh!" Her breath exploded out, pushed out by his entry, his size. His balls slapped against her pussy as he yanked her back against him, setting up the same forceful, driving rhythm with which she'd teased him earlier.

Oh, God. Her hands gripped the rail as he hammered into her, never slowing. Each thrust stretched her; each thrust increased her pleasure. He leaned over her back and captured a breast in one hand, and her pussy with the other. His fingers circled her clit, his thumb following the same movements on her nipple, and electricity zinged back and forth between her breasts and her clit until her hips jerked uncontrollably against his hand. Her vagina clenched around his shaft.

He slowed, moving his cock inside her in small circles, the head pressing into different places until he seemed to hit something different, and she rocked up on her toes as a surge of intense pleasure made her gasp.

"There, huh?" he growled and started thrusting again, only each time he hit that area, over and over. His fingers rubbed against her engorged clit in the same rhythm, inside, outside, and everything coiled inside her, tighter and tighter. Her legs stiffened, her butt arching up toward him, and she went totally still, afraid to move and lose that edge of ultimate pleasure where every stroke thrilled through her and yet pushed her inevitably over the cliff.

She screamed as the orgasm erupted through her in mind-shattering shudders. He didn't stop moving, his cock still striking that place inside her, and she came again before the first had finished. Her muscles went weak, and her hands fell from the railing.

He wrapped his arm across her hips, and his hand cupped her breast, holding her on her feet. Holding her for his pleasure. His strength kept her immobile as he thrust into her, ever deeper, until he growled his release, and the jerking inside her set off little explosions in her vagina, making her body clench and shudder.

He held her against him for a minute, his breathing fast, and she could feel his heartbeat where his wide chest pressed against her back. "Who needs fireworks when I have you?" he murmured into her ear. His teeth closed on the long muscle down the back of her neck, and she quivered uncontrollably.

With a soft laugh, he pulled out of her, making her moan, then set her like a doll back onto her blanket as he went to dispose of the condom. Beside her, she could hear the other couples—the rhythmic sounds of sex, the murmur of voices.

When he came back, he turned the chair sideways and lifted her into his arms, cuddling her against him. From there, with her head resting on his chest, she listened to his heartbeat and watched fireworks light up the sky.

* * *

Where the fuck was she? Kyler pounded on Elizabeth's apartment door again so hard his ring bit into his knuckle. No answer. No lights were on inside.

All the work he'd done this morning to finish up his caseload would be wasted if she didn't show up.

He walked across the asphalt in front of the building to the parking area. The first look shot panic through him. Her truck was gone. But then he saw her trailer, and his muscles loosened. She hadn't run.

Hell, he wasn't thinking clearly. This was a holiday after all. She'd probably gone on a date. *With another man*. Anger burned through him like spilled acid. "Fucking bitch." He slammed his fist on the wood of the trailer. Splinters dug into his hand, the pain snapping him back to reality.

Turning, he took deep breaths, forcing himself to calm down. Sweat beaded on his face and poured down the middle of his back as he walked away from the trailer. His anticipation had been so high, but really, this didn't change the plan he'd devised this morning.

Last week, his strategy had been to sedate her with valium and take her home right away. But now, his wait had been too long, and his anticipation had grown too high. He felt twitchy, off-center. He needed the release that only she could give him as he watched the look on her face when the whip struck, listened to her screams. Spilled her blood.

In the sky above the city, fireworks rose into the sky, the distant booms setting the air to throbbing. Damn her, where was she?

* * *

As the subs dressed, Nolan waited for Beth by the front door. The sound of giggling drifted from the powder room, and he grinned. Dan's Kari was not only sweet, but she had a wicked sense of humor.

And Beth… God, he loved hearing her laugh. He wanted to hear it more.

A minute later, she appeared. Seeing him, she walked over and looked up at him, obviously feeling a bit awkward now. "I had fun today, Master."

He smiled at the sound of his title from her lips. The foyer lights seemed too bright for what he wanted to ask, so he stepped outside. The humid night air wrapped around him pleasantly. He was hoping to have something—someone—else wrapped around him soon. "I did too. And I'd like to continue. Spend the night here with me."

She actually took a step away from him. "Sir…"

He leaned a shoulder against the doorframe, an empty hole forming in his chest. Having her in his arms had been the happiest he'd been in a long time, and he'd thought she felt the same way. To see her retreat from him now was like a fist in the gut. He couldn't keep the growl from entering his voice. "Do you really think I'd pound on you the way the bastard did?"

"No. No, my husband is a—"

"You mean your ex-husband, don't you?" Yeah, he'd figured she'd been married to the guy.

"Ah…yes." But her eyes flickered. She continued, "You're nothing like…"

He lost the rest of what she was saying as ice slivered up his spine and jabbed shards into his brain. "He's not an ex. You're still married to him," he said slowly. All the time he'd spent with her, been inside her, and… "You're a married woman, and I've been *fucking* you." He deliberately chose the coarse word.

The color drained from her face, leaving her golden freckles a muddy gray. "No, I-I…" She held her hands out to him.

"And you're lying." Just like his wife had lied to him. *I wouldn't cheat on you. Nolan. How can you say that?* As fury roared through him, he pressed his shoulder against the wall, knowing if he moved, the anger would erupt into shouting. His family tended to yell when upset, but he couldn't. Not now. To see her cringe from him at this point would be the last straw. He closed his eyes and sucked in a bitter breath as his carefully laid framework crumbled. Nothing can stand if not built on solid ground.

When he opened his eyes, she hadn't moved. What did she want from him? A noise came from behind him, and he glanced around. The others had entered the foyer and, from the look on their faces, they'd heard. "Cullen, would you see Beth to her car, please?"

Cullen hesitated. "Ah…are you—"

"Now, please."

Cullen's face tightened. "Sure, buddy. I'll do that."

"Thank you." Nolan stepped out of the doorway, keeping his face calm despite the fire roaring inside him, burning half-formed dreams into ash. "Thank you all for coming. I'm glad we could spend the evening together."

Kari took Dan's hand, glanced at Beth, and murmured, "Thank you for having us over, Nolan."

Cullen moved finally. He squeezed Nolan's shoulder, then gave Beth a small push to get her moving and jerked his head at Deborah to follow.

Once in the yard, Beth looked at Nolan over her shoulder, her lower lip trembling.

His return look kept her silent. “Goodbye, Beth.”

Chapter Twelve

Most people would get drunk right about now, Beth thought. She propped her chin on her knees and stared at the waves rolling onto the sandy beach. Over the past few hours, the tide had changed, leaving more and more of the white sand exposed. In the sky, black clouds were blotting out the stars. The increasingly gusty wind sent frothy spray into the air, and Beth's skin felt sticky with salt and gritty with sand. It didn't seem to matter.

How had everything gone so wrong, so quickly?

All her fault. She couldn't escape the memory of Nolan's eyes changing from a laughing heat to an icy cold that absorbed all emotions. His eyes had told her whatever relationship they'd had was dead and gone.

She heard the crunch of footsteps and turned her head to see a lonely beach walker skirting the water's edge. In dark clothing and in the tall grass, Beth wouldn't be easy to spot, but she patted her pepper spray anyway. She'd never been able to resist the ocean at night, here or in California, but she wasn't stupid, either.

At least about this. About relationships… How could she have been so stupid?

He might have been reasonable about her being married—maybe—but she'd killed everything by trying to lie to him. The one thing he had no tolerance for. Her eyes burned with tears, and she brushed them away. If she apologized and explained, would he listen?

His words didn't give much hope. "*Goodbye, Beth.*" That didn't sound much like a, "Call me and we'll talk about this." But what did she have to lose? And, okay, she knew he wouldn't want to talk to her, but she owed him an explanation. And thanks. God, she owed him so much.

Surely she could manage one phone call without crying and embarrassing them both.

Pulling her cell phone out of her pocket, she started to punch in his number and stopped, staring at the clock on the tiny screen. Four o'clock in the morning? He was already angry. Waking him up at this hour would be insane. She tried to laugh and failed, then dialed again, a different number on the West Coast. Her night-owl mom would still be up at one a.m.

"Mom?"

"Bethy. Oh, honey, I'm so glad you called." Her mother's voice, usually so warm and cheerful, sounded strained. "I tried to reach you earlier."

"What's wrong?"

"Now don't get upset. It might be nothing, and I might be just a paranoid old woman, but… Well, I went to the Gilmore's house for their Fourth of July party, the usual big bash. One of the Thompson girls was there. You remember the Thompsons; they live across the street from me?"

"Uh-huh." She didn't, but she knew now. "Go on."

"Emily came home in June for a bit before summer school started. She's at UCLA, studying to be a lawyer. Can you imagine?"

Beth rolled her eyes. Driving or talking, Mom had never met a detour she wouldn't take. "So what did Emily have to say?"

"Oh, right. She said she saw a man going through our mailbox. Last month."

Beth's hand tightened on the cell phone. "Going through how?"

"Well, she didn't see him all that clearly, but it sounded like he was flipping through the envelopes. He didn't take anything, so she didn't worry too much about it."

Beth forced her words out through a constricted throat. "What did he look like?"

"Blond. Thirties. A suit. Lean. It could have been Kyler." Her mom drew in a shaky breath. "I've been worrying ever since she told me, but you didn't answer your phone. I left you a voice mail."

Beth saw the little envelope on the cell phone screen indicating a message. "I didn't even check." She tried to speak, but couldn't find the air. She heard Nolan's voice. *Breathe with me.* One breath. Two. Her voice worked again. "So if Kyler found one of my letters to you, he might know I'm in Tampa, but he won't know where." Thank God she'd rented a post office box here.

"What are you going to do?"

She didn't have much choice, and the sudden upwelling of grief choked her. Leave her business, her apartment, her new friends? Leave Nolan? *Oh, God, why now?*

But if Kyler knew she was in Tampa, sooner or later, he'd find her. "I'll leave. I have to leave." Beth bit her lip, trying to keep her voice steady. Mom was upset enough. "I've always wanted to see what New England looks like. I'll try there."

"Oh, Beth, I—I could… Oh, I hate that man!" Her mother stopped, steadied her voice in just the same way Beth had. Weren't they a pair? "Be careful, honey. Be careful."

"Don't worry, Mom. I'll call you tomorrow." Beth flipped the phone shut and laid her head on her knees. The first sob welled up, and her throat was so tight it strangled inside. The second escaped as a ragged sigh, and then she cried. Ugly, painful sobs she couldn't hold back. It wasn't fair. Not fair! She had a life, friends… Nothing. She had nothing now.

Her eyes had swollen almost shut by the time she stopped. Her nose was clogged, her head aching. Of everything she was going to lose now, the one that made her heart twist the most was losing Nolan.

Only she'd already lost him anyway.

Knowing the futility, she punched in his number anyway. She just wanted to hear his voice one last time, that was all. But the phone rang and rang, then clicked over to voice mail. "This is Nolan. Leave your message now." Her lips turned up even as tears spilled over again at the sound of his deep gravelly voice. And his message, so terse and commanding. So Master Nolan.

Before she could stop herself, she opened her mouth and told him how sorry she was. Tried to explain…everything. Not that anything she said now would matter. By the time he listened to his messages, she'd be gone.

* * *

Nolan finished off his second beer and dropped the bottle into the bottom of the canoe. With a sigh, he watched the moonlight break into fragments on the small waves across the lake. The water lapped quietly against the boat as frogs chirped on the banks. Peaceful sounds; peaceful place. A pity his mind was at war. Over the course of the long night, he hadn't been able to negotiate a truce with the two arguments battling it out inside him.

She'd lied to him. No question. She was a married woman, cheating on her husband and willing to lie about it. Only a fool would trust her.

But he had. He tried to rub away the pain centered in his chest and wondered if he were having a heart attack. Hell, a heart attack would be easier. At least eventually that would come to an end. This pain wasn't going to go away anytime soon.

Her betrayal hurt. No two ways about it, he felt betrayed. As her Dom, he'd known she still had secrets, and eventually they would have explored them. Together. And in the process, he would learn more about himself. It was a two-way street.

Every sub he'd known—every woman he'd known—had hidden areas she didn't want to reveal… *She hates dark places because her mama locked her in a closet once. Her first lover told her she tasted bad down there, and that's why she hates oral sex. Her breasts aren't sensitive at all, but she fakes it because she thinks all sexy women have sensitive breasts.* Trying to unearth those mysteries was one of the pleasures—and frustrations—of being a Dom.

But this wasn't a secret; it was deliberate deception. Leaning forward, he rested his forearms on his knees, staring across the water and scrub forest to the west. One by one, the stars winked out as clouds piled up on the horizon.

Beth had known how he felt about adultery. He'd made his opinion very clear. Why hadn't she backed off or at least told him?

Because she knew he'd have been gone so fast her head would spin? Had their relationship mattered that much to her? He dropped his head in his hands and groaned. Of course it had.

He had mattered that much. He wouldn't feel like this if she felt nothing in return. Yeah, they'd had something going between them. But she'd lied and wiped it all out. *Damn her.*

Fine. It was done. He could return to picking up a sub for an evening, and she would…find someone to top her? The thought punched through his chest like a bullet. He'd have to watch someone else take Beth. See his hands on her, put himself in her. And watch her respond? Nolan heard roaring in his ears, and his hands fisted.

He shoved the pictures from his mind, concentrated on the waves brushing against the canoe. *Bad, Nolan, very bad.* He'd never felt that kind of jealousy with his wife. Hadn't felt it earlier today, but that was because Beth had belonged to him then; she'd been his to share for her enjoyment and his. But not anymore. Seeing her at the Shadowlands with someone else… He could feel his self-control shred at just the thought.

How could he never want to see her again and still want her so badly his muscles strained to go after her? He knew she'd destroyed what was between them, yet his mind kept flashing back to her face: white, eyes stricken, lips trembling, shoulders hunched. Every cell in his body wanted to protect her from the man who'd made her look like that.

He huffed a bitter laugh. That man would be him.

Nolan grunted at the slap of guilt. This was hopeless. His mind was going in circles like a rowboat with one oar. Picking up the paddle, he struck out for his dock. The wind gusted over the water as he paddled, and he looked up. The setting moon glowed an evil red through black clouds that now covered half the sky. In the east, the first glints of sunrise streamed through the palms, soon to be blotted out.

* * *

Beth's overloaded suitcases sat in the trailer. She'd filled supermarket boxes and stacked them by the door. And she still wasn't done packing. She'd accumulated more stuff than she'd realized. A pot here and a picture there, an African violet here, and a pillow there, all added up. She needed more boxes.

Her curtains glowed as the early morning sun hit them. Standing in the center of the apartment, Beth stretched and blinked her gritty eyes. No rest, a lot of crying, a lot of packing. She'd be lucky to not fall asleep on the road.

All right. She needed to get more boxes. Finish packing. See the apartment manager. She could notify the utility companies once she had gone; that at least could wait. Maybe it was silly to be so antsy, considering Kyler had discovered she lived in Tampa last month, but everything inside her kept screaming at her to run.

She'd almost just headed north straight from the beach, leaving everything behind.

But she couldn't afford that. She would need the garden service tools in the trailer and all the household stuff she'd bought over the last year. It would take every penny she'd saved to start over. *Again.* Her chest felt like someone had coiled a band around it, and she shook her head. No more crying. Not until she was gone.

She picked up the cell phone lying on the kitchen table and sighed. She kept looking at it every few minutes, hoping it would ring. That Nolan would have received her message. That he'd call. Pretty dumb.

The quiet knock on her door filled her with joy. *Nolan.* Dropping the phone, she ran to the door, flung it open.

"Elizabeth, my dear." The fist hit her face so hard she felt the skin on her cheek split against his ring, and then she hit the floor. Dazed, she fought back blindly, fists flailing away. One connected, and he cursed. Something bit into her thigh. A needle, she realized, struggling to sit up. He hit her again, knocking her flat. His foot came down on her chest, his weight pressing her down. She struggled helplessly for breath.

And the edges of the world caved in and sucked her into blackness.

* * *

Nolan walked into the kitchen, toweling off his hair. He hadn't tried to sleep; that would have been a worthless effort. But pounding on the bag in his workout room had eased the anger, and a hot shower cleared his mind. Nothing would help the hollow feeling deep in his chest.

As he poured a cup of coffee, he saw the message light blinking on his answering machine. He grunted. The way his life was going, probably one of his new office buildings had collapsed. He flicked the switch and leaned against the counter to listen.

"Nolan. Sir. I was going to call you. I mean I was going to call you before and try to apologize, only now…" Beth's voice. Thick. Wavering.

He set his coffee down slowly, feeling like someone had stomped on his chest. She'd been crying…was still crying. His guilt layered higher, brick by brick.

"Now I'm saying goodbye too." He heard a shaky breath. "And I'm not making sense. God, I'm sorry. I'm sorry I lied to you and made you… I shouldn't have let you f-fuck me once I knew how you felt about married women."

He winced at the word. Bad enough he'd used it, worse that she could apply it to an act that had been much more than just sex.

"But I couldn't get a divorce. I ran away. He'll kill me if he finds me; that's how my fingers got broken, from the last time. So I couldn't... But I should have told you."

With the sound of her sob, he stalked across the kitchen. The need to wrap his arms around her and comfort her was a burning knot inside.

"But it doesn't matter; nothing matters now. Mom said Kyler knows I'm in Tampa, so I have to leave, and I'll never get a chance to make this right." A sniffle, silence. "Anyway, I just wanted... I wanted to thank you. I wanted more time with you. I..." A gulping sob. "Be well, Master."

He stared at the machine. Surely she had more to say, hadn't just hung up. *Dammit, say more!* He slammed his hand on the counter next to the phone, making his coffee slosh over the side of the cup.

A sick feeling grew inside him. *What had he done?* Damn his blindness. He'd known her last lover, husband or not, was the one who'd beat the crap out of her. He'd known the bastard had scarred her mentally and physically. He'd known she'd probably run from him. And filled with self-righteous crap, he'd come down on the little rabbit like a truckload of bricks.

How the *hell* could he blame her for doing anything she needed to ensure her own safety? "*He'll kill me if he finds me.*" She'd done what was necessary to survive.

Fuck... He felt like she'd slapped him upside of the head with a two-by-four instead of a phone call. He snorted. Being Beth, she hadn't been trying to change his mind. She'd just wanted to apologize and say goodbye.

What did he want?

He scrubbed his hands over his face. *Face it, idiot.* The little sub had gotten to him with that combination of fear and trust, of passion and innocence. With her love of beauty and her willingness to work like a dog to achieve it. With her growing need to please him and her surprise when he cared for her in turn. And fuck it all, he wanted to continue to care for her and protect her. Did he love her?

Maybe.

He would have liked a chance to find out, but he'd screwed that up rather badly. *No kidding, asshole.* He'd overreacted and behaved like a man seeing his home fall apart in front of his eyes. But it hadn't been the whole house. He'd barely begun to build really. And yes, the foundation had been laid on ground that was too soft, on a lack of knowledge and fear and untruths, but there were ways to stabilize all that.

He could rebuild. They could rebuild.

If she wanted to. He remembered the way her eyes had looked when he said goodbye. Stricken. Lost. He'd never forgive himself for being so fucking cruel. But could she forgive him? That was the question.

Apparently she planned to very politely take herself out of his life. He hit the counter again. Here she goes and rips his heart into pieces and then thinks she's going to just up and leave?

No, not just leave—run. He set his jaw. She planned to run, to let her bastard husband win when she had him to defend her? *Like hell!*

* * *

What a pit, Kyler thought as he wiped rain from his face before unlocking the door to the tiny cabin. But, as the realtors always said, location is everything.

He turned and smiled in satisfaction at the surrounding area. Trees, palms, and palmettos stretched out into a dense green jungle. The only way to the cabin was a tiny dirt road and the only sound he could hear was rain pattering on the tin roof. No traffic, no neighbors. *No witnesses.*

He glanced at the rental car where Elizabeth slumped against the door, still out cold. Just as well. He needed time to set up. The thought sent excitement through him, and he hardened.

He shoved the door open. A yank on the string turned on the bare bulb hanging from the ceiling. Quite a dump. A faded couch sat across from the door. To the right, an ancient mattress lay on the floor in one corner and a wood stove with a chipped brick hearth occupied the other. On his left was the gourmet kitchen: an avocado-colored refrigerator, a dirt-encrusted stove, and a chipped enamel sink. He sneered and winced as pain lanced across his face.

Touching his nose gently, he winced. One lucky punch and she'd almost broken his nose. Damn her.

He glanced down at his bloodstained shirt. At least he had a change of clothes in his carry-on. Along with a nice set of tools he'd bought in Tampa. Turning, he smiled at the ugly room.

The cabin was isolated and big enough to swing a whip. What more could a man want?

Chapter Thirteen

Nolan pulled his truck into the parking space next to Beth's. The relief of seeing her truck and trailer let him take his first decent breath since he'd listened to her message. He wasn't too late.

Stepping out of his truck, he noticed two suitcases wedged between the mower and brush cutter in her trailer. So she had been serious about running. Dammit. He stalked toward her apartment then slowed. Little rabbits frightened easily; he'd need to go easy. Not roll right over her with…

Her door was ajar.

He nudged it open with his foot. "Beth?" An edgy feeling crawled up his spine and raised the hair on his scalp. Over the last year in Iraq, his instincts had become as fine-tuned as when he'd been slitting throats for the CIA. Head up, body tensed, he reached down and drew the knife from his boot sheath.

Remaining in the doorway, he scrutinized the one-room apartment. Totally silent. Boxes on the stripped bed. Curtains still drawn and lights on. Pots and pans stacked on the counter. A canvas bag on the small kitchen table, cell phone beside it.

Dark spots just inside the door on the beige carpet. He bent, touched one lightly. Wet. Red. He sniffed. *Blood.*

* * *

"Wake up, darling. Time to play."

Beth heard the voice, her mind moving like sludge, still thick with nightmare images. She didn't like that voice and couldn't remember why, but the sound made something inside her wail in terror.

If the voice wanted her to wake up, then she wouldn't.

She let her breathing stay long and slow, kept her body limp, and her eyes closed. She fought to stay awake, and lost the battle. But something was very wrong…

* * *

"What happened?" Frowning, Z walked into Beth's apartment. "And give me more than '*Beth's been grabbed.*'"

Seated at the kitchen table, Nolan glanced up, a moment's relief running through him. Reinforcements. "Got a message telling me goodbye, said she was leaving because her husband—the bastard who gave her those scars and who she escaped from—found out she was in Tampa." He smothered a growl. "When I got here, the door was open. Car and trailer in the lot. Purse, cell phone here on the table. Blood there." He nodded at the stain on the carpet.

Z touched the blood. "Still wet." He glanced around. "This looks bad."

"Yeah. How the hell do we find her?" Nolan scrubbed his face with his hands. "I don't even know where she came from or where her husband lives."

"California," Z said. "She let that drop one day."

"That helps. To get back there, he'll have to drive or fly. Either way, he'll probably use his credit card."

"Do you know her husband's name?" Z walked around the cabin, checked the chest of drawers.

"She said *Kyler* on the message. But she's smart. She'd have changed her last name." Nolan tapped his finger on the table and then grabbed the cell phone lying on the table. "Somebody else might know the bastard's name though." He found the phone's contact list and arrowed through the entries. "*Mom*. That's promising."

A minute later, he had a hysterical woman screaming in his ear. "Ma'am, please. We're looking for her. I need to know her husband's name. His legal name." He pushed the button for the speaker phone.

"Kyler Stanton. It's Kyler Stanton. Please, he's a horrible man. He'll kill her." The woman was crying so violently, she choked.

"Listen to me," Nolan ordered, knowing just how she felt. Damned if he didn't want to put his fist through the wall. "Your daughter is important to me, and I *will* find her. Can you trust me to do that?"

Her sobs slowed. "What is your name?"

"Nolan. I'll call you when we find her." He flipped the phone shut.

Z was already on his cell phone. “This is Zach. I need to know any credit card activity for a Kyler Stanton. Especially in the last day or so and especially in Florida. I’ll explain later, but I need it stat.” He listened, and then snapped, “I’ll wait.”

Nolan raised his eyebrows.

Z gave him a faint smile. “Give Dan a call. But my ex-military, old-boy system might be more efficient than the cops.”

Nolan paced across the apartment. Stopped and looked down at the blood stains. His gut twisted. “They’d better work fast.”

* * *

A brutal hand struck Beth’s face, and her eyes snapped open.

“Ha! I knew you were faking.” Kyler’s blue eyes gleamed. “You’ll pay for that, Elizabeth.”

Kyler. No nightmare. Her breathing increased so quickly that the world started to blur. *Breathe, sugar.* The memory of the deep voice anchored her. Nolan would never panic. She forced herself to inhale slowly and looked around.

She lay on a filthy mattress on the floor. Kyler stood over her, smirking, and the hate that blasted through her at the sight of him cleared her head. His nose was puffy, discolored, and she felt a rush of satisfaction. She’d hurt him. She tried to keep from showing her satisfaction. And failed.

“Yes, you bitch. You managed to hit me. Once.” Mouth thinned in a line, he slapped her again. She lifted her hands to fight back, only to see handcuffs on her wrists. The metal cuffs were hooked to a chain dangling from the cabin ridgepole. He'd cuffed her ankles together too. Terror burst inside her, and she screamed over and over until Kyler's enjoyment registered. She stopped, her chest heaving, and closed her hands to hide the trembling.

"You don't know how much I've missed hearing you, my dear." He ran his hand over his groin. "Look at that. Already hard as a rock." He paced across the room.

They were in a cabin, she realized. A tiny one-room cabin. Rain thundered against a metal roof. "Where are we?" she managed to ask, her tongue dry and thick.

"In the country where the only things listening will be the alligators and herons."

"Someone will hear." She didn't sound convincing, even to herself. "There are hunters everywhere. You'll get caught."

He turned to show her a cheap pistol tucked into his slacks. "Don't worry your pretty brain, my dear. I did take precautions. It's amazing what a person can obtain with a little money. Buying a weapon in Florida is even easier than in California."

Her heart sank.

"I never imagined you'd run so far." He smiled, stroking himself through his tailored slacks. "I almost gave up on finding you. I tried going to prostitutes, but they didn't excite me like you do, no matter what I did to them. I crippled one so badly I doubt she lived. She screamed, nice and high, but she wasn't you." His eyes held a weird light, a wrong light.

Beth's stomach turned over. He was completely insane.

"I need you, Elizabeth. Just you."

Her breath hitched as panic rose inside her. She'd told Nolan she was leaving. Her mother wouldn't expect to hear from her right away, not for a day or so. The cabin was in the country with no one around. *Oh, God. Don't panic. Think.* "Listen, Kyler," she said. "You don't want to hurt me right now. How will you get me back to California if I'm all bloody?"

His laugh escalated, going higher and higher until she cringed from the sound. "I chartered a private jet. I told them you were in a car accident, but you're crying to go home to Mommy. I'll dope you to the gills, stick you in a wheelchair, and roll you onboard. They'll think I'm the best husband in the world, pampering my injured wife."

His plan would work. Oh, God. She closed her eyes, breathed through her nose.

"So, since you're awake, let's get set up."

She tensed. Time to fight. But rather than coming closer, Kyler walked across the cabin and picked up a chain. Dismay filled her. The chain, attached to her wrists, went through a massive eyebolt in the ridgepole, and Kyler had the other end. As he dragged on the chain, it lifted her up until she dangled from her arms, her feet on the mattress. The metal cuffs burned as they cut into her skin, tearing open old scars.

Kyler tied the chain in an elaborate knot to a hook buried in the wall and looked at her. "Look at that. Just where I've been imagining you all these months." He faced her toward the wall.

She heard him rummaging in a bag. Her teeth clamped together at the snap of his whip.

"I was going to start slow and work up to the good stuff, but I just can't wait." The whip sliced across her shoulders, the sting lessened by her shirt. At first. Until the whip sliced the fabric to ribbons.

Then the real pain began.

* * *

Hoping the pounding rain would drown out the sound of the engine, Nolan didn't slow as the truck tore down the dirt road, fishtailing through the curves, bouncing through the deep ruts. Z braced one hand on the dash and stayed silent. Finally the truck broke out of the forest into a small clearing that held a tiny, ramshackle cabin. A white Taurus with rental plates was parked in front. "Got you, you bastard," Nolan muttered.

Not daring to get any closer, he left the truck at the edge of the clearing. "Take the back," Nolan muttered to Z and headed for the front door.

Just as he reached the cabin, a high scream cut through the noise of the rain and sent rage searing like fire through his body. One kick took out the door, leaving it tilting from one hinge.

Beth hung from her cuffed hands, a bloody slice across her stomach, her eyes glassy with pain. Even as his fury increased, relief spread through him. Alive. She was alive. She saw him and blinked. Frowned. Her lips formed his name. *Master.*

Nolan turned his attention to the fair-haired bastard standing in the center of the room, a knife in his hand.

"This is a private party. Please leave." The man sounded as if he'd been interrupted at a dinner function.

"Let her go," Nolan said, circling. How good was the bastard with a knife?

"She's my wife, and she's going nowhere." The man's eyes narrowed. "You're the one who walked her to her car at the club. The one who kissed her."

Nolan could see white around the guy's pupils. The fucker was seriously nuts, and he had a knife. But angry fighters make mistakes. Pissing him off would even the odds. "Yes, I kissed her"—Nolan curved his lips into a gloating smile—"and more. She's one hot little woman."

"You fucked my Elizabeth? Inside her?" A howl burst from the man, but rather than attacking, he backed up. Reaching behind him, the guy hauled out a pistol.

Fuck. Knowing he was dead, Nolan charged across the room.

"No!" Beth screamed. Dropping all her weight on her cuffed hands, she lifted her feet and kicked the bastard in the back.

The pistol fired, a sharp blast of sound and a *crack* as the bullet hit the wood floor. Nolan slapped the weapon out of the guy's hand and punched him hard enough to feel ribs break.

The bastard landed on his back, holding his side, and wheezing. And laughing.

Pulling back his foot for a kick, Nolan hesitated. What was so funny?

"You can't win, you know." Tears were in the man's eyes as he lay on his back, not even trying to rise. "I hear sirens."

Nolan could too. He glanced outside. Not in sight.

Silently Z eased past the broken front door and headed for Beth. The place had no back door, Nolan realized. He looked down at the asshole. "The cops will lock you up for a long time," he prompted, wanting to see where the guy was going with this.

"And I'll be out soon enough. I'm a lawyer. Rich. I'll destroy you, and I'll have her in the end. And she'll pay for letting you touch her." A flash of rage crossed the man's face. He sat up, holding his ribs. "You did this for nothing."

Nolan studied him for a moment, his mouth tightening. The bastard was telling the truth. *Kyler was crazy. He was rich. And he wasn't going to stop.* The bottom line was that Beth would never be safe.

Nolan glanced at Z and saw the same conclusion in his expression. Z nodded. Coldness slithered up Nolan's spine as his mind opened the door to his past.

So be it.

Beth shook her head and roused again at the sound of sirens. She could feel blood trickling down her arms, her back, and her stomach, and yet the pain was absent. And Kyler had stopped. With an effort, she focused her eyes and saw a man trying to unfasten the chain from the hook in the wall. *Master Z?*

Another man stood in the room, towering over Kyler. *Nolan.* He really was here. This wasn't a dream. She watched as Sir's expression changed, cold replacing anger. When he stalked toward her ex, Beth shook her head. *No, no, no. Don't trust Kyler.* No matter how big Sir was, he could still get badly hurt.

"I hardly did this for nothing," Nolan said to Kyler with a sneer. "She has a pussy worth taking. Yeah. Honey sweet."

With an ominous whine, her husband pushed to his feet, and Beth whimpered. *Don't hurt Nolan.* She turned to Z over at the knotted chain. "Help him," she whispered. "Please."

Z's silvery gaze met hers. He shook his head.

He wouldn't help? What was *wrong* with him? She tried to yank free, and pain seared her wrists.

"You touched her." Kyler's mouth twisted. "She's mine. My wife."

"Hell, she doesn't want to be married to a wussy like you. She wants a man."

Beth screamed as Kyler launched himself across the room. At the last minute, Sir stepped out of the way, and Kyler staggered to a stop almost at the far right wall.

"You know how good she sucks cock?" Nolan chuckled, and Beth stared at him in shock. Was he insane?

Kyler attacked again and hit Nolan in the face.

Sir grinned. "One more please." And took another fist against his cheek. He shook his head like a bull shaking off flies, before hitting Kyler, forcing him back a step. Kyler groaned and attacked again. Blocking a fist, Nolan punched Kyler in the ribs where he'd hit him before.

With a howl of agony, Kyler folded over. Beth saw Nolan inhale, his muscles bunching, and then he hit her husband squarely in the jaw so brutally that Kyler flew backward. The back of his head slammed into the wood stove with a gut-wrenching *crack*, and he dropped onto the brick hearth.

Beth heard a roaring in her ears as she stared at the man lying on the floor.

When Nolan bent over him, then turned away, she tried to warn him that Kyler would jump up and hurt him…to watch out, only she couldn't seem to find any air.

The chain holding her jerked, and she moaned and tried to muffle the sound. *Don't wake him up; he's just sleeping.* Nolan came across the room to her, and she shook her head at him. *No, watch Kyler. Watch him.* Only Sir wasn't listening.

As Z lowered her, Nolan held her steady and then lifted her into his arms. His arm hurt her back, and it didn't really matter. She turned her head to watch Kyler. *He would hurt Sir. She had to keep him from hurting Sir.*

"Beth." Master's deep voice. "Look at me." He turned so she couldn't see Kyler.

She raised her head and met eyes so black and fierce, she cringed.

"Easy, sugar. It'll be all right. The ambulance is almost here."

She realized she was whimpering. Sir held her closer, his hard grip reassuring. This wasn't a dream; he really was here. And she tried to tell him how she felt since he always wanted to know, but once she started, she couldn't stop whispering one thing, over and over, "You came… You came… You came…"

He shook his head at her. "Shhh." He tucked her head against his chest and with Z's help shifted her so his arm didn't rub the open areas on her back. Z searched the cabin for the handcuff key.

Had Kyler gotten up? She tried to look over Nolan's shoulder, to watch for him. An ambulance appeared outside the broken door. Maybe they'd take her husband away, and Nolan would be safe.

Z appeared in front of her. "Hold on, little one. Let me get these off." He unlocked the cuffs, carefully easing the metal out of her mangled flesh and swearing in a voice she'd never heard before.

When one place hurt too much and she whimpered, Nolan growled low and deep. He scowled at Z. "I want to kill him again."

"Get in line."

* * *

The world was a muddled place, filled with pain. Sirens. Men's voices. The sharp smell of antiseptic. Rocking and bouncing that made everything hurt. Humid air. More pain.

When Beth finally managed to open her eyes, she was surrounded by white curtains. A familiar sight. She was in an emergency room. Left with strangers. She let herself fall back into darkness.

She roused again at the sound of a low, commanding voice, one that washed the loneliness away.

A woman's voice raised in frustration. "I'm sorry, sir, but family only."

"I am family." Sir's voice came closer. "Beth, which cubby are you in?"

"Um." Did they have numbers for white-curtained rooms? "Here. Wherever that is."

"But—" the woman sputtered. "Oh, fine. Obviously she wants you with her."

A scarred hand pulled back the curtain, and Nolan entered, taking up all the extra room. His gaze took in the blood pressure monitor on her arm, the IV bag dripping fluids into her. "All the essential equipment, I see."

She'd felt all alone and helpless, remembering how the paramedics had looked at her with pity. An abused woman covered with scars. No one saw *her.*

Until now. Sir leaned over the hospital gurney and looked into her eyes. "You want company, sugar?"

Her eyes brimmed with tears, and she could only nod.

"Good answer. You saved yourself a fight." He leaned an arm on the side rail and picked up her hand, engulfing it within his long fingers. "Did they give you anything for pain?"

"I told them no."

His brows drew together. "And why would that be? You're hurting."

"I… Kyler gave me something to knock me out. And pain medicine makes me fuzzy. I don't… I can't handle not being alert right now."

He nodded. "Good enough."

A doctor came through the curtains, a lean gray-haired man with sharp blue eyes, stethoscope around his neck, flipping through pages on a clipboard. "Mrs. Stanton?"

She cringed at the sound of that horrible name, and Nolan's grip tightened. She took a breath. "Yes."

He ran through the standard medical questions, ones she was all too familiar with from her frequent emergency room visits. If she'd been too badly hurt for Kyler to fix, he'd take her to the ER, different ones each time to prevent questions. When her scarring got too obvious, one doctor suspected abuse and tried to get her to a shelter. Kyler had pulled strings—his family knew everyone—and she'd not only been released to Kyler, but she'd been punished for arousing the doctor's concern.

"All right then, let's see the damage," the doctor said now. He helped her sit up, opened her gown, and started peeling off the gauze dressings the medics had applied. She concentrated on staring at Nolan's hand covering hers. He had a scar there on the knuckle and another on…

The doctor made a sound. Beth looked up. His lips were pressed so thin, they were white. "Who did this to you?"

"My husband," she said.

The doctor's gaze settled on Nolan. "You?"

"No. Her husband's dead."

The doctor looked at the bloody gauze in his gloved hands. "Sure he is. How long's he been dead?"

The curtain whipped back. "About an hour." A heavy man in a dark suit walked to the foot of the bed and flashed a police badge. "That about right, Mrs. Stanton?"

"I…" How long had she been out? "I don't know," she said, feeling helpless.

"You want to tell me about your day?" He pulled a notepad from his pocket.

"You want to wait until I sew her up?" the doctor snapped.

"Actually, I'd like to see the damage before you do that," the cop said. "The guy at the cabin"—he glanced at his notes—"Zachary Grayson said the husband whipped her. Now that seems a little—"

The doctor not only stepped back but shoved the cop into his place where he could see her back. "Ah"—the cop cleared his throat—"hell. He sliced you up good, didn't he?"

"Breathe, sugar," Nolan rumbled, his watchful eyes on her.

She sucked in a breath.

"While you're here," Sir ordered the cop, "look at the older scars too. She ran from him a year ago. He found her again this morning."

"Ma'am, I'm sorry," the cop muttered. "I saw the chains and handcuffs, and I figured some kinky games, not… Jesus, I've never seen anything like this." He stepped away from the bed, his ruddy face almost pale. He looked at her. "Anything else besides the whip marks?"

She swallowed. Why did she feel humiliated when it had been done to her? "There—"

"Scars around her wrists." Nolan held up her hand where a bloody gauze dressing circled her wrist. "Those scars are pretty well wiped out by this new damage. Cigarette burns on her left breast, some knife scars on her bottom, old broken right leg, puncture wounds on her hands, and broken fingers." He rubbed her fingers where shiny white spots marred her tan. "The doc here can probably document all that for you when he examines her."

The cop's face had gone rigid during the recital, but his eyes softened when he looked at her. "How many times did you try to get away?"

"Just once before last year." She stared down at her hands. "That was when he smashed my fingers."

The doctor sucked in a breath but didn't speak.

A muscle twitched in the cop's cheek as he looked down at his notepad. After a second, he asked, "So today, you have a cut-up back. Anything else?"

Nolan spoke for her again. "From today, she also has a slice across her stomach from a knife. That's when Z—Zachary—and I got there and stopped him. I broke the door down. He had a gun, tried to shoot me, and although chained, she managed to kick him from behind." Nolan gave her such an approving look that she warmed all the way through. "The bullet went into the floor. We fought." He touched his cheek and chin from where Kyler had hit him. "I hit him, and he fell back against the wood stove."

"How do you know Mrs. Stanton here?"

"She does yard service for Zachary. I was going to hire her for my place and ended up dating her instead." He kissed her palm then gave her a merciless look. "But you're still going to have to landscape the place, sugar."

She actually managed to smile at him and touch his warm cheek, although her fingers trembled. "I think I owe you that now."

"Looks like a pretty clear case of self-defense," the cop said. "Give me your name and address and all that."

Nolan took out his wallet and fished out a card.

The cop glanced at it. "King Construction? You built the office complex down the street from our station."

Nolan nodded.

The cop studied Nolan for a minute. "You're military too, aren't you? Like your buddy, Zachary. A vet?"

Nolan nodded again.

"No wonder. Nice work," the cop said. "And you didn't hear me say that. I'll be in contact if I have more questions." He walked out, shaking his head.

"Questions. They always have questions, always need more evidence." The doctor scowled and raised his voice. "Marilee, bring me the camera."

The nurse popped in a second later.

"Stay here as a witness, Marilee," he said. "Let's go ahead and document this clearly, just in case there's any question down the road." The doctor's face was grim. He snapped pictures of Beth's back, then taped up the whip marks and sewed up the ones too deep to butterfly or glue shut. More pictures on her front, and he sewed up the slice across her stomach. His exam was thorough, and he took a picture of every scar, from her hands down to her leg.

Through it all, Nolan sat quietly, holding her hand, and murmuring when something hurt.

As the doctor wrapped her wrists with gauze, Master Z walked into the cubicle.

"What is this, Grand Central Station?" the doctor snapped. "Who the hell are you?"

Beth actually giggled. "It's all right. He's the other one who saved me."

"Well, fine then," the doctor grumbled. He shook hands with Z, then grinned and looked from him to Nolan. "Good job, guys, and I don't care who hears me say it."

Nolan barked a laugh.

"Now then, I'm releasing you. Come back here or see your doctor if there's any sign of infection. I'll give you a prescription for pain—"

"I don't want one," she interrupted. "I won't take them."

"Ah. All right." He rubbed his chin. "Tylenol or ibuprofen. Avoid aspirin for a couple of days. The nurse will be in to get you unhooked from the IV and give you instructions about the stitches."

Shooed out by the nurse, the men waited in the parking lot for her. When the nurse wheeled her out, they helped her into Nolan's truck.

"Are you all right, little one?" Z asked as he took the seat belt from her and fastened it.

Her friend count had been a little low, she thought, but seemed to be rising rapidly. She smiled at him. "I'm very much all right. I feel like I've been caught in a blackberry tangle, and someone just cut me free." Her eyes filled with tears as she whispered, "Thank you so much."

He actually grinned. "No problem, although Nolan had all the fun. Now go home and work on healing." He rubbed his knuckles over her cheek. "You can expect to see Jessica soon."

As the truck started, he glanced at Nolan. "Are you taking her to her apartment or—"

"She'll be at my house," Nolan said flatly.

"Excellent." Z nodded and closed her door.

"Nolan..." Beth started. He shouldn't have to take care of her. "I can go to my—"

"Don't bother to argue. We're both going to have nightmares. You will be in my bed and in my arms when that happens."

Nightmares. He was going to have nightmares? Oh, God, he'd killed a man for her. She took his hand. "You killed him. I'm sorry, so, so sorry."

He looked at her blankly before snorting. "I don't have nightmares from killing cockroaches, sugar. But knowing he had you...hearing you scream...seeing you all bloody? Now that's going to bother me for a long time. And you're going to have to stay with me till it doesn't."

"All right." She couldn't think of anywhere else she'd rather be. It seemed wrong to hope he'd have nightmares for at least three or four days, but—

He put the truck into gear. "I figure in a year or two, I might be okay."

Chapter Fourteen

Standing in his kitchen, Nolan stared at the little sub and managed to keep the growl out of his voice. “You’re what?”

“I’m moving back into my apartment.” Beth took a step back, then crossed her arms and raised her chin.

The signs that she was getting back to normal pleased him, but she sure as hell didn’t have to go this far to prove she was feeling better. It had only been a couple of weeks. *Reasonable. Be reasonable.* “Why the *hell* would you want to go back there?” He winced at the snap in his voice.

She bit her lip, then stepped forward and wrapped her arms around him.

He held her close and rested his cheek on the top of her head, remembering how she’d hugged Cullen. Did he look that bad? “Okay, sugar, tell me why.”

Her arms tightened. “I need to know that I can live on my own. I-I love being here with you, and I don’t want to go, but I have to.”

“Gutsy rabbit.” He could understand the need. He’d grown up in a family that firmly believed in the “face your fears” technique. But how did a man deal with the need to stand in front of a little rabbit and protect her from those fears?

"Not all that gutsy. It's just, well, if I stay with you because I'm scared to be alone, well…that isn't much of a relationship."

She had a point. He wanted to ask her what kind of a relationship she thought they had, but didn't. After meeting her sick fuck of a husband, he wasn't about to put any pressure on her. When she was ready to let him know how she felt, she'd tell him. Although it felt like he might be old and gray before that happened.

He rubbed his cheek in her soft hair and inhaled her strawberry fragrance. He'd have to get her to plant a bed of strawberries so he could mash them against… "You know, I have a lot of kinky things I still want to do to you. You gonna be available?"

She giggled, a husky chuckling sound that lifted his mood. "You're the Master. All you have to do is tell me to be, right?"

Wasn't it a shame it didn't really work like that. His power over her lasted only as long as they both wanted it to, and no longer. "Well then." He could feel the healing scabs under her shirt and could feel how tense her muscles were. Going back to a place she'd been attacked couldn't be easy. Maybe he'd just help her over the first hurdle. "I have a craving to see how loud I can make you scream in a tiny apartment. You have an apartment I can use tonight, sugar?"

Under his fingers, the long muscles of her back slowly loosened. "You know, I just happen to have one available." She rubbed her forehead against his shoulder and whispered, "Thank you, Master."

* * *

Nolan glanced at the cage in the corner. The male sub looked miserable but in no real physical distress. He strolled past and down to the next station where a Dom was securing his sub in the stockade. Tears already ran down her cheeks although the cane at the Dom's feet hadn't been used yet. She'd probably be a screamer.

Nolan stopped to scan the crowd around the door and the bar. No Beth yet. Where the hell was she?

A lesbian couple with the sub in saloon girl garb and the Domme in a very risqué sheriff's outfit walked past, and Nolan eyed the sheriff's bare legs appreciatively. Old West Night at the Shadowlands was one of his favorite themes; he was Texan, after all.

He shoved his Stetson back and slowed to check the whipping post that Z had brought out just for tonight. Using a whip in the main room meant roping off extra space to keep from nailing spectators by accident. Dressed in outlaw black, Sam had Deborah tied to the post. Nolan stopped to enjoy for a minute. The old sadist was a real master with that black snake whip of his. Deborah was already up on tiptoes and well on her way to subspace.

Nolan scanned the room again. No Beth. He'd planned to pick her up, but she'd called to say she was running late, and Z had asked him to monitor the main room. Well, if she got cold feet, he'd just have to go out to her apartment and fetch her. *That fucking apartment.*

She'd been living there for a week now and damned if he didn't miss her more than he thought possible. He'd joined her for her first two nights there, and then had let her go it alone. Sure, he still saw her every day, joining her for supper or lunch, occasionally tossing her onto that miniature apartment bed and fucking her senseless. But he wanted her back in his home, padding around in one of his shirts that dwarfed her, arguing with him about how strong a pot of coffee should be, draping that trim little body over him while they watched the evening news. Her laughter…her teasing…her enthusiasm… When she'd moved out, his house had turned as gloomy as if winter had arrived.

He wanted her back.

Did she want to come back? She wasn't sharing how she felt. Gratitude, sure, she didn't have a problem telling him all about that.

But what she felt for him was a hell of a lot more than mere gratitude. He knew that. Did she?

Or was the little rabbit just having trouble getting the words out? Talking about her feelings still came hard to her. Of course, it was a Dom's duty to help little subs past mental blocks like that.

So…

Another scan of the room, and he found her. He grinned, pleasure filling him at the sight. Now that was an outfit. High-heeled black boots, black leather chaps, a shiny blue G-string. The fringe from a matching blue bustier danced over the creamy skin of her stomach and concealed the fading pink scar. Her hair was in two stubby braids.

Nolan glanced at his watch. His time had been up for a good ten minutes. Then again, Olivia never showed up on time. He spotted the Domme at the bar, caught her eye, and tapped his watch. She nodded and sauntered over to take the flashlight from him.

"No problems," he told her.

"And you have things to do." Smirking, she slapped his shoulder. "I saw your sub come in. She looks hot."

He grinned and gave her a warning look at the same time. "Mine, Olivia. Hands off."

"Oh, I already tried hands-on a month ago. She doesn't walk on my side of the street… More's the pity."

Ben had liked her outfit, Beth told herself as she moved toward the bar. The thought didn't help much. Her stomach still felt like she'd swallowed a mess of worms. Knowing her abuse was common knowledge made her feel more exposed than stripping her clothes off and walking around naked.

And yet, she'd missed being here, missed the driving music, the sound of sobbing and whips, sex and pain. The scent of leather and latex and perfume. And the costumes tonight… She grinned in delight. Even the most conservative of Doms—the ones who wore suits—had added cowboy hats. The majority of subs favored saloon girl outfits, some of which mixed oddly with spiked green hair and Goth makeup.

The appreciative glances coming her way bolstered her confidence as she searched for Nolan. Surely he'd be done with his dungeon monitor chores by now. Not in sight. Dodging around various groups of people, she made her way to the bar.

Cullen spotted her and abandoned whatever drink he was making. "Little Beth!" He leaned a muscular arm on the bar, and his warm gaze ran over her. "You look good, love. Wish I'd been there to lend Nolan a hand."

She smiled at him, pleasure running through her. Another friend. "Thanks, Sir. Can you tell me where Master Nolan is?"

"Turning over his DM duties to the compulsively late Olivia." He tilted his head. "Want a drink? And this time tell me what you'd really like. I bet it's not a screwdriver."

"Irish whiskey. Bushmill's single malt if you have it."

He roared a laugh. "Pint-sized sub takes her liquor straight, hold the water. Coming right up, pet."

After he set her drink in front of her, she sipped it slowly, enjoying the smooth burn.

"Hi." A man in black latex jeans and a long-sleeved latex jacket slid onto the bar stool beside her. "I haven't seen you here before. Are you new?"

"Not exactly."

A hand closed on her bare arm. She almost jerked away before she recognized the grip. Nolan.

"Now here's a cute little western girl," he said softly. His dark eyes heated as his gaze ran over her, lingering on her G-string. "Well worth the wait."

She felt her insides melt at just the sound of his deep voice and the look in his eyes. She touched his cheek with her fingertips. After all the Doms she'd had, only this master could make her feel like an eager puppy, wanting simply to please him.

Cullen walked over and set a Corona on the bar. Nolan started to pick it up but frowned and picked up her glass instead. He sniffed it. His eyebrows rose. “Well, you’re just full of surprises, sugar.”

“She’s hard-core, buddy,” Cullen said, grinning. “So do I get a bar decoration tonight?”

Beth stiffened. *God, no.*

“Nope,” Nolan drawled. “I’ve got other things in mind. While you’re here, give me some ice, would you?”

Cullen nodded and moved away. A few seconds later, a glass of ice slid down the well-polished bar.

Nolan looked at the man who’d tried to start a conversation with her. “I’m Nolan. You new here?”

“I’ve only belonged a couple of weeks.” They shook hands. “I’m William.”

Sir rested his hip on the barstool, pulling Beth back until she could feel his big erection against her bottom. Her body flared to life at the feel of him, at the memory of what he felt like inside her. They’d made love almost constantly when she’d lived with him, and she’d missed it. As she leaned back, his arm wrapped around her, keeping her tight against him.

“So are you enjoying yourself?” Nolan asked the Dom as he plucked an ice cube from the glass with his free hand. He ran it casually down Beth’s neck and across the top edge of the bustier, making her nipples peak, before playing in the fringe over her stomach.

“Ah.” The Dom’s eyes were glued to the ice moving over Beth’s body.

She'd have laughed, only her mouth had gone dry. She started to move only to realize Nolan's embrace trapped her right arm against her side, and his hand gripped her left wrist in an immovable grip. The ice traveled lower and paused above her G-string long enough for freezing water to trickle over her mound. She jerked as the cold hit her hot flesh.

"Ah, right. Yes, everyone is very friendly," William said, his voice a little rougher.

"Good."

As the ice melted, Beth held still, wondering what the man would do to embarrass her next. And why his actions turned her on so much. Dammit.

Seeming to have read her mind, he started unhooking her bustier one-handed. She tried to pull her wrist from his grip. "Don't move, sub," he snapped, and her body froze.

"Have you met some of the subs here?" Nolan asked the other Dom as his fingers continued to undo the hooks.

"Um. Yes. No. I guess not." William shook his head, took a step back and, with visible effort, raised his eyes to Nolan's face.

When Beth's bustier fell open, Sir cupped her breasts. "You know, most of the unattached subs sit over there." Nolan took one hand away to point to the nearby sitting area.

William turned to look, and his eyes widened. "Really? I thought they were already taken."

"Nope. If a Dom leaves his sub over there, he'll chain her, so there's no question about her availability."

"Damn. Now that's good to know." William gave the subs an assessing look, and she could see that he might be a decent Dom after all. He had that… She gasped as Nolan pinched her nipple, making both her breast and her clit throb.

"You have the prettiest breasts," he murmured in her ear, his thumbs rubbing over the peaks. "And I brought decorations for them." Reaching into his pocket, he pulled out a pair of nipple clamps, held them up in front of her. Tweezer-type like before, these had little bells at the end.

Oh, man. Quivers woke inside her in anticipation of the pain…in anticipation of the excitement.

He turned her around and attached one, watching her face as he moved the little ring up to tighten the clamp. As the pressure grew from stimulating to painful, he stopped and loosened it slightly. He did the other the same way.

"All right?" He studied her.

She wet her lips as the pressure in her nipples sent erotic messages to her clit, making her even wetter. And when he flicked one bell, making it tinkle, a surge of need shot through her.

"Definitely all right," he murmured with a slow smile. He rang the other bell, one hand on her upper arm to keep her from moving away. "You know, I'd planned to play at the bondage table, but I just remembered this very interesting rope job I saw in the dungeon. On the sling."

His thumb stroked her mouth, slid inside, and she sucked.

"I saw a great way to tie a sub, legs up and bent so"—he bent and whispered in her ear—"you're very, very open to anything I want to do."

A wave of heat ran through her, and she bit his finger.

With a chuckle, he moved his hand and put his arm around her waist. He said to William, "I've been considering getting a sling for my dungeon. Might as well test-drive one here."

"Don't waste your time," said a man in an ugly voice.

Beth stiffened. The Dom she'd picked up last month when hoping to avoid Nolan stood beside William, sneering at her. "She looks pretty, but she's frigid as an iceberg. And dry as the desert."

As William gaped, Beth turned her face away, not wanting a confrontation. After all, the Dom was right; at least, that's how she had been for him.

She felt Nolan's arm flex then relax. "Really?" Nolan's voice sounded like he'd eaten gravel for breakfast. "Interesting similes, I'd have to say. Now me… I found her hotter than the desert, and when all that ice melts, it leaves her really wet." His arm around her waist firmed to keep her in place as he slid his free hand under her G-string and through the wetness there. She quivered, trying not to move. After holding up his glistening fingers, he put them in his mouth. "Mmm. Nothing like it."

The Dom's face reddened. Mouth set in a nasty line, he turned away and came face-to-face with Master Z.

Master Z's eyes had the color and warmth of slate, and although his voice was soft, the anger in it cut like a blade. "Donald. I would like a word with you. Now."

The Dom turned pale.

So did William. He gazed after the two men. "Whoa. I don't know Z that well, but I've never seen him look like that."

Nolan pulled Beth in front of him, her back against his chest. Wrapping his arms around her, he kissed the top of her head. "Being angry at a sub because a scene goes bad or you don't get the response you want isn't the mark of a good Dom. And insulting a woman for any reason is the mark of an asshole."

William nodded. "I agree with you there." He smiled at Beth, glanced at Nolan. "I'm going to grab one of the subs over there. It was nice meeting you two."

"Have fun," Nolan said, then squeezed Beth affectionately until the air hissed out of her lungs. "Come, little rabbit, I hear a sling calling your name." He grabbed his toy bag from behind the bar and towed her behind him through the crowd to the back of the huge room and then down the hallway to the dungeon.

When they entered, most of the stations were in use. On the far left and right, subs hung from manacles embedded in the rock wall. Near the back, a Domme on the queen's throne rested her feet on a beefy sub. The bondage table was empty. In center left, a male sub was suspended head-down, being whipped by his Dom. In the very center, a brunette sub stood on tiptoes straddling a pony board. From the way her legs were shaking, her legs would soon give out, and all her weight would press her pussy down on the edge of the board. Beth winced in sympathy.

Center right—a full body, leather sling with embedded D-rings, suspended from a rafter by four chains. Beth had never used one before, and she eyed it with a mixture of anticipation and worry.

Nolan glanced at the observers scattered around the dungeon, then looked at her. "Sugar, kneel beside the sling."

Her heart sped up, knowing he'd gone into full master mode. He watched her with an impassive face as she knelt, and her bustier flapped open. She knew better than to try to close it. She looked up, caught Master's frown, so she parted her legs more and set her hands on her thighs. And sighed. Once upon a time, taking this position would blank her mind until she didn't care what happened. But with Sir, she cared. Every sense was alive, and her body was on edge.

He cleaned the sling thoroughly although the last user undoubtedly had also. From his toy bag, he pulled out long silk ties and hemp rope. Her stomach twisted. He was planning to restrain her. He hadn't done that since the day Kyler abducted her. His gaze fell on her. "Breathe, sugar."

She pulled in a breath.

"Come here."

She walked over to him.

"I want the G-string and chaps gone."

Biting her lip, she stripped her lower half, setting everything next to his toy bag.

"And the bustier."

She shrugged out of it. Hands around her waist, he lifted her onto the sling, and the cold leather chilled her bottom. She wrapped her hands around the chains as the sling rocked.

His eyes kindled, and a smile softened his harsh face. "You look very pretty there," he murmured. "Like a wartime poster of a naked woman on a swing." After tossing his hat onto his bag, he patted his pocket where Beth could see the outline of a pair of scissors. After folding the hemp rope in half, he wrapped her, below her breasts, over her shoulders, between and then above her breasts, pulling until the rope squeezed snugly without being painful. She looked down. The ropes formed the outline of a square bra with no cups, pressing her breasts out from her rib cage.

"Never experienced *shibari* before?" He flicked the bells on her nipple clamps, making her moan. "This fast little configuration is called *shinju*."

As the sling rocked, she wrapped her hands around the chains, but he shook his head. "Lay back, Beth."

Why did lying on her back feel more vulnerable than on her stomach? Yes, she'd much rather be on her stomach. Glancing at Master Nolan's face, she saw no chance of being given a choice. She let herself sink back. The sling was surprisingly comfortable, almost like a hammock. She looked over at Sir, and her gaze was caught by the sight of her breasts, standing up like little mountains.

Gripping her hips, Sir moved her butt down to the edge of the sling. He tied one of the silk braided ropes across the top of her hips, over the top of her mound, pinning her bottom to the sling. Using more silky ropes, he lashed one ankle about two feet up the chain and did the same on the other side.

When he finished, she lay on her back with her ankles fastened high on each side, her knees bent and in the air. Hell, he'd turned this into a rocking gyn table. Only with her hips directly under her feet, she was way more exposed than any medical table.

From the murmurs of the people around the room, they appreciated Sir's rope job much more than she did.

Not that he'd notice his audience. His attention was completely on her. Studying her expression, he ran his hand down the inside of her thigh, sending shivers through her. "I really like this position," he said, a slight smile on his face, and the enjoyment in his eyes warmed her. His finger slid through her wet folds, and she inhaled sharply. "Look how open you are."

He gave the sling a push, letting it rock while he walked over to the wall. The winch turned with a clacking sound, and the sling rose until she swung at chest height. Way too high for him to use his cock.

Her hands gripped the chains beside her shoulders. He hadn't restrained her hands, she realized. Maybe if she didn't move, he wouldn't remember.

He walked around the sling to kiss her, taking it deeper, harder, forcing her response. By the time he pulled back, her fears had disappeared under the wave of heat. Smiling, he flicked the nipple clamps. The bells tinkled, tweaking her breasts, sending hot need burning from her breasts to her clit. Her fingers tightened on the chain, catching his attention, and she stiffened. *Please, no restraints.*

Pulling her hand free, he nipped her fingers before curling them back around the chain. “I’m not going to bind your arms, sugar. You’ll feel better knowing they’re free, but I don’t want your hands to move from the chains. Am I clear?”

“Yes, Sir,” she whispered, able to smile at him as relief surged through her.

“Good girl.” He strolled back down to the foot where the V between her legs was spread wide for everyone to see. Her nipples burned from the clamps, and now he stroked her legs, moving closer and closer to her pussy and to where her clit throbbed in cruel need.

Chapter Fifteen

Nolan smiled at the sight before him, Beth's body stretched out and open, quivering with urgency and anxiety. Her eyes were wide, her fingers clenched around the chains. Her breasts, swollen and tight, stood up proudly from her chest, the peaks dark red from the nipple jewelry. He smelled both strawberries and her arousal as the sling rocked gently. His gaze dropped to her pussy. The swollen labia opened widely and pointed to where her clit peeked out from under its hood. Begging for him.

It wouldn't be the only thing begging shortly. He'd placed her at just the right height for his fingers and his mouth. He bent slightly and ran his tongue up through her folds. Her inhale was louder than the dark music of Rammstein coming from the speakers.

He toyed with her, stabbing his tongue into her vagina to enjoy her taste, circling, then running up and over her clit. He used his fingers to open her even more, holding her labia apart and tonguing her bared clit until the muscles of her thighs tensed and her hips tried unsuccessfully to lift.

He moved away, leaving the swing rocking and Beth squirming in frustration.

Pulling on a latex glove, he lubed his fingers generously. Rimming her back hole with a finger, he spread the cold lube. He chuckled when she tried to jerk away only to discover how well he had her lower half restrained. Setting his finger against her anus, he slid in a quarter of an inch.

Eyes widening, she struggled and got nowhere. "No!"

"Oh, yes." He pushed his finger in farther.

Oh, God, he had his finger in her ass. Slick and cold and such a strange feeling. Nerves she hadn't felt before started to fire as he eased out slightly, then in farther. "No..." she moaned. Having him touch her there was too intimate, left her too vulnerable. She'd never let anyone do this to her before.

The thought of using her safe word crossed her mind, and then his mouth came down on her clit, sending the sensations there instead. But as he moved his finger, in and out, the tiny fucking motions sent need rioting through her body. Tongue, finger, tongue, finger, her mind couldn't process the sensations, and her whole lower half tightened, more and more.

He pulled his finger out and pressed two against her, right at the very entrance. Her anus clamped shut, refusing admittance. He waited, flicking his tongue over her clit, his touch too gentle to give her release, driving her mad with impatience. She tried to lift her hips, and the inability to move drove her higher again.

Then his tongue came down on her clit, rubbing it in a demanding stroke, right over the top, the sides, the top, and she was almost...almost... His two fingers drove into her rectum in one hard stroke, and she broke with a scream of shock, the waves of sensation tangling together in her lower half, shooting electric blazes through her whole body. Her pussy tried to buck against his lips, and nothing would move. She could only lay there and shiver, and come and come and come.

As she shuddered with the aftermath, he moved away, disposing of his glove. He returned to lean on the side of the sling, rocking her slightly. Still stunned from the way he'd made her climax, she just watched him, content to have him close. People moved around the room and were undoubtedly watching. She couldn't bring herself to care.

His fingers toyed with the jewelry lying on her breasts, making the tiny bells chime. "You know," he said in a musing tone of voice, "I think you've started to get off too easily." He bent and licked over one clamped nipple, his tongue hot. He blew over the wet peak and smiled as she shivered. "From now on, you need to wait for permission to come."

"What?" she asked in disbelief. During the party as part of the game, that had been bad enough. But here in the club? She could barely get off. Well, before Sir, she could—

He grasped her chin and commanded, "You don't come until I say you can. Is that clear?"

"But…but what if I do? Master?"

"Then you will have disobeyed me."

Oh, God. She stared at the heavy rafters above her and tried to imagine not coming when his mouth was on her. Or when he was in her, so big and thick. Just the images alone made her wetter. Try to hold an orgasm back? Her vagina clenched.

He tugged on a nipple clamp, jerking her attention back to him with a rush. "Time to take these off. You ready, sugar?"

Before she could yell no, he'd unfastened the first one. Blood surged back into the nipple. *Pain. Ow, ow, ow.* She sucked in a breath, her hand starting to—

"Keep your hands on the chains, sub."

She hissed with the erotic agony, the intense sensation almost pleasure but not quite. Before she'd recovered, he did the other one. Her hands clenched around the chains. He wet his finger, rubbing each peak. Pain and pleasure twined together, the sensations way too intense. She shut her mouth over the moan.

"Very pretty." He gave her a hard kiss. "And you kept your hands on the chains. Good girl."

He walked back around to his toy bag and started rummaging in it. She couldn't see, dammit. Finally he returned, back between her legs. He put lube on something. Oh, that wasn't good. She craned her neck. He met her gaze and held up a butt plug. Her mouth dropped open.

"Just a little bigger than my two fingers," he said. "Now that I know how excited you get, I'm looking forward to taking you that way too."

That way? Like anal sex? Master Nolan was huge. Her back hole contracted as if in protest. "You're too big," she whispered.

"That's why we're starting off with this size." He smiled at her, ran his finger down her clit. "Tomorrow you can have a size larger." Without waiting for her response, he slid the thing right into her.

"Ahhh!" She jerked against the restraint.

His hand pressed down on her mound. "Now did that hurt...or feel good?" His dark eyes studied her.

"It's okay." It was sending tingles through her, just from being inside her. She wanted, needed to wiggle, and his hand held her in place.

"Beth," he warned.

Her lips flattened. She didn't want stuff stuck up her ass, dammit. But it felt good. *Dammit.* "Good," she admitted.

"That's my honest sub." His slow smile warmed her as it always did. He walked to the wall and with a rattle and clinking sounds, lowered the sling until it stopped about the level of his hips. She shivered, knowing what would be coming next, only there was something inside her...

But he came back to the middle of the sling, bent, and started kissing her breasts. They were swollen and tight from the ropes, making everything he did more intense. He worked his way up to her nipples, and at the first touch of his lips on the excruciatingly sensitive tips, she squeaked. He ignored her, firming his lips over the nipple, laving the peak with his tongue, the sensations painful, then pleasurable. Even the pain sent erotic jolts straight to her clit. Warmth pooled deep within her. He teased first one breast, then the other, back and forth until she arched up and her hands pulled on the chains.

When he stopped, it took her eyes a minute to focus. By then he was between her legs, sliding his fingers through her folds, rolling her labia between his fingers, spreading her wetness over her clit. With a grin, he squirted lube on her stomach and chuckled as her stomach muscles flinched at the cold sensation. She couldn't imagine what he needed lube for. The anal thing was already in her, and her pussy was embarrassingly wet.

He unfastened his leathers. Pulling a condom out of his pocket, he sheathed himself. His eyes had turned to molten darkness, and he was hard, very hard as he pressed himself against her, easing in slowly as he watched her face. He kept thrusting, unrelentingly. With that thing inside her, and now him, she felt overfull, stretched beyond comfort. When he stopped, he was deeper than he'd ever been before, and her insides throbbed.

As he pushed the sling outward, she shivered, starting to enjoy the full sensation, and she wasn't too worked up this time to enjoy it. The sling rocked out and back, moving him inside her until her vagina felt as if it was swelling, becoming more sensitive. The anal plug moved inside as his cock pushed it out of the way, and each thrust jostled the nerves inside her rectum, sending new messages sparking across her pussy.

"Feel good?" he asked, eyes on her, a crease down one cheek.

"Oh, yes."

He chuckled. "Not good enough if you can still talk." He gripped the bottom of the sling, just under her right hip and kept the rocking motion going. Watching her face, he took a finger-full of lube and set it right on her clit. She shuddered as the cold sensation shot through her like an electrical storm. And then his fingers, slippery with lube, slid over and around and on top of her clit, dropping her past need into true urgency. Her hips strained upward, her hands clamping on the chains.

Each firm stroke over her clit drove her inexorably closer, and his cock inside her piled sensation on sensation, coiling her tighter and—

"Don't come, sugar," he warned in a low voice. "You don't have permission." But his fingers didn't stop moving.

She gritted her teeth, trying to shove her climax back, trembling with the effort, even as he rocked her faster, impaling her on his cock. Harder and harder. He abandoned her clit, grasping the chains with both hands, yanking her onto him, letting her rock away before pulling her back right onto his massive cock, again and again, and each thrust sent her higher. Her whole body shook with the need to come, and she moaned, "Siiiir..." She panted as her world narrowed to each unimaginably intense thrust, as if she could feel every tiny micrometer of him entering.

Then he slowed, holding the sling away from him. His cock teased at the lips of her empty vagina. Her pussy felt as if it were on fire, burning with the need to come. He rocked the sling sideways, his cock sliding horizontally across her folds, not nearly enough to satisfy her. Why was he doing this to her?

"I decided it was time we had a little talk."

"Are you serious?" Her voice sounded as if someone was strangling her.

"Very." His look turned obstinate. Ruthless. His cock edged up to slide across her clit, reawakening all the nerves.

She waited for more… Nothing. "Wh-what are we talking about?"

His cock probed her entrance. She wanted to push herself down on him and couldn't move an inch.

"About our relationship. Tell me how you feel about it."

He wanted conversation? "Besides wanting to kill you right now?"

His grin was a flash of white in his bronze face. He rocked the sling side-to-side, never entering her. And waited.

Her legs quivered. "Um." How could she think about this now? Relationship… Just thinking about the word made her feel unhappy. She'd told Kyler she loved him, and he'd used her. She didn't want to love anyone again. Sir's dark gaze captured hers, and she wanted to touch him, run her hands over his face. Yes, she cared for him, really, really cared for him. But it wasn't love. She wouldn't let it be love.

"You love me, sugar. I know that." His words thudded into her like painful blows to her chest. "Can't you say the words?"

"I…" Her arousal was dying as confusion, and worry filled her. He knew she loved him? Her hands tightened on the chains until her fingers hurt. Yes, she loved him; how could she not love him? But telling him would leave her so vulnerable. "I can't."

"All right." His eyes never left hers. "Then say, 'I don't love you, Sir.'"

The thought of saying that, the sheer wrongness drove the breath from her lungs. Her eyes filled, and she shook her head helplessly.

"You, little rabbit, are very good at getting yourself stuck where you can't go forward or go back." His eyes crinkled. "Let's see if I can't give you a push." Setting the head of his cock at her entrance, he rocked the sling, each movement sending his cock into her a little farther. And when he was fully inside her, he leaned forward over her. Now his hips alone rocked the sling. His pelvis rubbed on her mound, and the anal plug moved inside her, and suddenly her whole pussy was stabbing with need. His hands cupped her rope-tightened breasts, and his thumbs rubbed over her very tender nipples.

Abruptly, she was close to coming. Very close. She panted, arching her breasts into his big hands.

And then he stopped. Completely.

"Oh, God," she whined. "Please, Master. Not again." Everything down there throbbed, leaving her on the excruciating edge between pain and ecstasy.

He jiggled the sling slightly, and she moaned.

"I love you, Beth. Do you love me?"

What had he said? Her body froze, all the sensations suspended in time as her brain tried to process his words. He loved her? *Loved. Her.* Oh, God. Warmth filled her chest as she stared at him. "Me?" she whispered.

Despite his sigh of exasperation, a crease appeared in his cheek. "Do I look like I'm fucking someone else in this sling? Yes, you. My little rabbit. My sub. I love you, Beth."

He'd said the words again. With her name, they had even more impact. He knew her better than anyone ever had, seen the scars on her body, on her soul, knew her fears. He'd let her snap at him before her period, complain when he ate the last of the bread. She shook her head, tried to see a lie in his eyes and saw only love. Right there, in his eyes, something she'd never seen before in any man's eyes. *Oh, God, he* did *love her.* The certainty stole her breath away, and her veins seemed to flow with sparkling bubbles as exhilaration filled her.

His smile grew slightly. "You're pleased that I love you. That's a start." His mouth firmed. "Do you love me?"

The joy of his declaration didn't make the words come to her tongue. Her mouth went dry. She tried to stiffen, but he moved inside her again. His fingers slid through the lube on her stomach and down her mound. Almost to her clit. Almost, almost…

"Can't you trust me enough to tell me this?"

"Oh, please…" He loved her. She loved him. *Why couldn't she say it?*

His finger drew little circles just above her clit. Nothing else moved.

"I want your answer now, sugar."

Her hips tried to wiggle and couldn't. Her thigh muscles were taut with trying to get closer. His finger never stopped, never came close enough. He moved inside. Just a little. "Say it."

Her mind couldn't cope with the overloading sensations and his implacable demand, and her defenses crumbled.

Tears filled her eyes, turning his face to a blur, and she choked on a sob. "I l-love you, Master. Sir. N-Nolan. I do," she whispered. Wetness spilled down her cheek.

"I know." His eyes were warm, his smile satisfied. His calloused hand gently wiped the tears from her face. "However, you will say that to me every day. So you don't get out of practice."

"I love you," she said again. The words came easier this time, and he grinned at her.

"All right then." Straightening, he grasped the chain and started rocking the sling. As if waiting had increased the pressure, her body shot straight to arousal. As his cock plunged into her, her clit rubbed against him with each thrust...her exquisitely sensitive clit. She trembled as her body coiled inside until every muscle hurt, her legs straining against the restraints. His thrusts grew hard and faster.

And then he pinned her with a steady gaze. "Come now, Beth." His lubed fingers slid straight over her clit and rubbed firmly.

She screamed, screamed, screamed, her back arching, the ropes tightening on her breasts as he thrust into her, rolling her into another orgasm. Before she could recover, he leaned forward, holding her breasts in his hands as he ground his cock deep inside her, jerking his orgasm as she spasmed around him.

Still deep inside her, he lowered his weight down on her, his body warm against hers. She wrapped her hands around his shoulders holding him to her as the sling rocked them gently.

After a while, he braced his elbows on each side of her and lifted his head, his black gaze amused. "So you love me, huh?"

"You…" she sputtered, ignoring the thrill the words sent through her. "You blackmailed me into saying that."

He grinned. "And I enjoyed every minute of it." He tipped his head down to lick her nipple, and she squirmed under him. "So did you lie to me, or do you mean it?" His gaze was no longer amused as he studied her face, his eyes intense.

She swallowed. *Can't lie to a Dom, not this Dom. Ever.* "I meant it," she whispered. "It's just so hard to say."

"I know." His cheek creased. "And I'm going to remember how well torturing you this way works."

Lord help her.

His big hands cupped her face. "You know that I love you, Beth. Come and live with me. Come home." He held her gaze with his, his body over hers. The scarred hands that had brought her back to life, saved her from Kyler, and brought her joy, stroked her cheekbones. He waited.

And she knew there was only one answer possible, one that came easily to her lips. "Yes, *Sir.*"

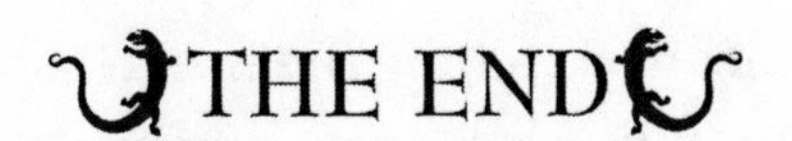

Cherise Sinclair

I met my dearheart when vacationing in the Caribbean. Now I won't say it was love at first sight. Actually since he was standing over me, enjoying the view down my swimsuit top, I might even have been a tad peeved—as well as attracted. But although our time together there was less than two days, and although we lived in opposite sides of the country, love can't be corralled by time or space.

We've now been married for many, many years. (And he still looks down my swimsuit tops.)

Nowadays, I live in the west with this obnoxious, beloved husband, two children, and various animals, including three cats who rule the household. I'm a gardener, and I love nurturing small plants until they're big and healthy and productive...and ripping defenseless weeds out by the roots when I'm angry. I enjoy thunderstorms, playing Scrabble and Risk and being a soccer mom. My favorite way to spend an evening is curled up on a couch next to the master of my heart, watching the fire, reading, and...well...if you're reading this book, you obviously know what else happens in front of fires.

Loose Id ® Titles by Cherise Sinclair

Available in print at your favorite bookstore:

Masters of the Shadowlands
(contains *Club Shadowlands* and *Dark Citadel)*
Breaking Free

Available in e-book format at www.loose-id.com:
Master of the Mountain
The Dom's Dungeon

The MASTERS OF THE SHADOWLANDS Series:
Club Shadowlands
Dark Citadel
Breaking Free
Lean on Me

LaVergne, TN USA
29 September 2010
198882LV00002B/83/P